The Skin Game

The Skin Game

And Other Atlantic City Capers

JOSEPH T. WILKINS

Library of Congress Number: 2002092478
ISBN: Hardcover   1-4010-6170-2
                    Softcover   1-4010-6169-9

This book was printed in the United States of America.

To order additional copies of this book, contact:
Xlibris Corporation
1-888-795-4274
www.Xlibris.com
Orders@Xlibris.com
15553

Dedication

To Mark who, with his brother, sisters, and mother urged me for years to get it down on paper.

Forward

The reader, being of sound mind and discriminating literary taste, will not mind a gentle reminder that this is a novel – a work of fiction, sprung from the fevered imagination of the author, and that any resemblance to any person, living or dead, is wholly coincidental.

Naturally, a novelist needs a certain poetic license to tell his tale in an entertaining fashion. But such necessary artistic liberties should never be taken seriously.

The reader can rest assured that every lawyer, judge, politician, public figure, citizen of and visitor to Atlantic City I ever met during the time covered by this book was honest, upstanding, reputable, virtuous and chaste. All the lawyers were scholarly and honest; all the judges were sober, learned and fair; all the defendants were presumed innocent. It's true that a number of folks were convicted of this or that offense but, as many of them insist to this day, they were undoubtedly framed, or were the victims of misleading impressions and circumstances.

The Author
Smithville, N.J.
May 10, 2002

Joseph T. Wilkins
P.O. Box 185
Oceanville, N.J. 08231-0185
e-mail: wilkins1@att.net
Tel: 609/703-5421

Chapter I

My name is Tim Donovan, and like every other name in this story it's been changed to avoid the laws of libel. Also to make damn sure I don't blow whatever cover I get from the statute of limitations for my sins.

Looking back over the slow-motion train wreck I call my legal career, I admit it wasn't the smartest time or the best place for a young lawyer to hang out his shingle. The place was Atlantic City, and it was the year Atlantic City hit bottom, before they legalized gambling (or "gaming" as the casino P.R. folks want us to say), and before the plain old Howard Johnson's became Caesars's Casino-Hotel. If you were looking for signs of economic life in the city, you could hold a mirror to its mouth all day and it wouldn't fog up.

"I thought I was the smartest guy in town," a business client groused to me one day. "Then I realized that everybody who wasn't an asshole left town, and all I am is the smartest asshole."

Civic outrage, never a prominent feature in Atlantic City's make-up, was equally dead. The State police raided the Loyal Order of Antlers for illegal slot machines and nobody blinked. The Mayor was sentenced to a 10-to-20 year stretch in federal prison and the whole town skipped to the sports page.

There were a few high spots, such as when the cops pulled their annual Christmas raid on Sonia's whorehouse – varying their normal routine that year by stealing her shoe box full of cash, which drew heavy criticism from old timers as unsportsmanlike conduct. Sonia was 76, the shoe box held her life's savings, and there are some things decent cops didn't used to do. The old Atlantic City of gentlemen's agreements and civilized theft was clearly dead.

And a guy in a ski mask walked into the Pelican bar and blew Eddie Kelhamp away in front of his wife, his bookie, and his bartender. The local lawyers wanted to put up a reward for the hit man. Not for his arrest. For him. Whacking Eddie did more to improve justice in five minutes than ten years of Bar Association meetings.

Eddie was a part-time municipal judge, juggling bribes on one hand and stiff sentences on the other. A fine legal scholar, as they say at all lawyer's funerals. I can vouch for that. One of my first clients was a suicidally depressed mother of five who headed up the Parkway with a bag full of uppers, downers, and enough reds, whites, greens and purples to open a jelly bean store on the Boardwalk. She found a quiet parking place in a rest area, gulped down pills by the handful, and turned on the radio planning to take life's exit ramp listening to happy tunes. But she fell across the seat unconscious, knocked the gear into Drive, and exited the rest area heading North in the Southbound lanes until she drifted off the road into the woods. The troopers found her with the motor running, lights on, radio playing, and half a dozen leftover pills scattered on the front seat. After the hospital pumped her stomach out, the prosecutor charged her with driving under the influence of controlled substances. In those days, if you couldn't pay the mandatory $200 fine, you went to jail to work it off at $5 a day. Having no bribe money to offer Eddie Kelhamp I argued that sending her to jail just because she couldn't pay the fine was clearly something no rich person would suffer. It was, I insisted, a clear denial of the equal protection of the laws guaranteed by the 14th Amendment.

As always when faced with a legal argument, Eddie sensed trouble. Raising his eyes first in puzzlement and then in anger at the thought that anybody failing to pay a bribe would expect justice, he lost the thread of my argument but retained his own sense of outrage. "The

Fourteenth Amendment to *what?*" he glared, his face and bald scalp red with anger.

Eddie's death improved the local bench, but not much. In one town Sam Roore, a gaunt, grey, miserable bastard, had recently sentenced an eight-month pregnant Puerto Rican girl who neither spoke nor understood English to 30 days in jail for taking lunchmeat out of one bag and putting it into another; a technical shoplifting offense. In another, goggle-eyed, hiccuping, permanently drunk Dave Robertson staggered and lurched onto the bench every Tuesday night – taking a break every hour or so to relieve himself. The firemen, whose latrine he used, regularly found him standing at the urinal, head leaning against the wall, asleep. They'd wake him up, and out he'd go to hear another drunk driving case.

And those were only the township judges. The county boys with life tenure were worse. Tom Rostenbach, for example, was a quiet, mean-tempered drunk who accepted a guilty plea from Arnie Seligmann to a charge of bookmaking (not the publishing kind), then accepted an ice-making machine as a gift from Arnie while the pre-sentence report was being prepared. When the Press asked the inevitably awkward questions, he stoutly insisted the gift was from Arnie in his capacity as an old friend, not in his new role as a criminal awaiting sentencing.

As I said, it wasn't the smartest time to go into the law business, and it sure as hell wasn't the right place. The only good thing you could say about Atlantic City was that it wasn't in Mississippi. Which is why, coming back from a week of skiing, I didn't bother to catch up on the newspaper. I came into the office that morning blissfully unaware of the trouble ahead.

*   *   *

Bob LeBreaux, the thin, elegantly dressed and hyperactive Public Defender sent me the case. It was, like most of the disasters that fill my filing cabinet, my own damn fault. After I left Legal Services and hung out my shingle, I'd asked him for some referral work to get jury trial experience.

"Hey, Tim," he said over the phone, "you still looking for trouble?"

"What's it pay?"

"Lousy and late."

"But it does pay, right?" I'd been in private practice two months. The $5,000 I'd borrowed to set up shop was already gone. My secretary, keenly aware of how few clients had coughed up any money, was getting nervous about payday. So was I.

"Yeah. Look – I've got a conflict case. Three guys are charged with sticking up the skin game and . . ."

"What's a skin game?"

"Card game. These guys are heavies that came down from Newark. My staff guy can only represent one of them. I gotta farm the other two out. Your man's got twenty-two counts of armed robbery, four counts of assault with intent to kill, six counts of assault with guns and intent to kill police officers, one count of possession of a pistol, and one count of possession of a sawed off shotgun. I'll send you the papers. Thanks."

"Wait a minute! Wait a goddamn minute! Why not send me Jack the Ripper, for chrissakes? This is my first jury trial!"

"Don't worry. I'll tell my guy to help you. Gotta go. Bye."

"No, no. Wait! What's my guy's name and where is he?"

"Frank Satterlee. He's in Mays Landing. Raffaelli put two hundred fifty grand on him, so you have to take a shot at bail reduction. I'll send somebody right over with the papers."

That the file was in my hands that afternoon should have alerted me to how desperate the Public Defender was to palm the case off on any sucker dumb enough to take it. But I was as desperate for money as he was for help. Little did I know how long it took the State to pay.

Chapter 2

It had been the back room of a store many years ago. The front room still boasted the big plate glass show window of times long gone. But on this night nothing of business remained in the front room, nor anything else except the old couch from which the deep snores of the lookout rolled out in a cadence of progression and recession that, had anyone bothered to think about it, matched the comfortable, lulling sound of the waves bringing in the tide on the Atlantic City beach three blocks to the east.

Neither the snoring of their lookout, nor the distant waves, nor the hot music from the Club Harlem across the street nor the impassioned argument between the man and woman in the front booth of Sapp's Fried Chicken next to the Harlem, nor even the occasional shout of greeting or insult that make Kentucky Avenue's nightlife so lively reached the group of intent black men in the back room. They were a quiet bunch, as befits men with serious money on the table waiting for the turn of the next card. Only half could sit at the table; the other half stood behind them, leaning over to get their bets down. Big Dingy, who would have made a perfect Buddha had he been cast in jade instead of ebony, was the dealer. He was not a man who encouraged idle chit-chat. Nor were the old-timers like Shipyard Slim or Cutie Boy much for small talk. As for the younger men, such as Elijah Morton and Riff, prison life had taught them there was a time to sow and a time to reap, a time to grieve and a time to rejoice, a time to talk and a time to play your fuckin' cards.

The game was Skin, played with four decks. Everybody drew a card and laid it face up on the table; four of clubs, ten of hearts, whatever. Big Dingy flipped over the deck, card by card. Your bet was that your card didn't get flipped. As each card was flipped, the dealer raked the bets of anybody having the matching card into the pot. The last man with an unmatched card got half the pot. The others got skinned. It lacked the casino elegance of James Bond playing Baccarat, but the spirit of the thing was essentially the same. Without, of course, the tuxedos and blondes.

Also missing was any greeting of new customers by the house management. When the five gentlemen from Newark pulled up to the storefront in a black late model Buick, no valet came to open their car door. The visitors didn't seem to mind. One stayed at the wheel. Of the remaining four, one leaned against the car, his hands inside his black leather jacket. Black was the color of choice that night. The car was black, the men were black, their leather jackets were black, and even the barrels of their several shotguns and pistols were, if not black, at least a dark enough blue to be hard to see in the dim light as the three remaining arrivals walked up the side alley to the door which led to the back room. Mr. Eddie Jones stayed outside by the alley door while Mr. Frank Satterlee and Mr. Calvin Williams made their entrance.

"All right, motherfuckers! Git your hands up! Now!" Frank brought his sawed-off shotgun out from under his coat and covered the crowd. Calvin Williams, a quiet man by nature, said nothing. He contented himself with motioning those already standing to turn around and face the wall. The motion was emphasized by his shotgun. The men turned and faced the wall. Frank ordered those seated to keep their hands in clear view on the table.

With quick efficiency, Calvin disarmed the standing men, relieving them of a surprising arsenal of guns, knives, and brass knuckles. These were kicked into a corner. Next came watches, cash, and diamond rings, which were tossed onto the card table, adding greatly to the pot.

That done, Calvin looked at Frank for instructions. "Strip 'em and stick 'em in there," Frank nodded to the bathroom. There was an ugly moment when the men debated whether to suffer the indignity of losing their clothes, or the inconvenience of being killed. When the first bunch had been stripped down to their skin and shuffled into the bathroom, Frank turned to those seated.

"Up, motherfuckers! It's your turn." Further instructions followed.

Having watched their colleagues and realizing that the bathroom was unlikely to be roomy enough to hold 20 or so men comfortably, no matter how naked, the seated players stayed put. Frank put his shotgun to the ear of the man nearest him, and started to count. When he got to "two" the man got up, emptied his pockets, removed his clothing, and joined his friends in the bathroom, never taking his angry glare off Frank's face. Frank did not seem perturbed. The other players quickly followed suit, except for Elijah Morton. Elijah, a veteran of a half-dozen armed robberies in which he had held the gun, had spent most of his young manhood in prison, where getting naked with other men was not the recreation of choice.

Feeling the need for direct action, Elijah miscalculated certain basic laws of physics regarding time and distance. He shoved back his chair, rose to his feet, climbed over the table, and tried to wrest the shotgun away from Frank Satterlee. In this he failed. Frank, with remarkable vigor, whacked Elijah alongside the head with the butt of the shotgun.

This would normally have ended the protest had not the shotgun gone off, blowing out an overhead light and encouraging Elijah's fellow card players to kick over the table and try to win justice for their side. Confronted by two shotguns and unwilling to die in the nude, they soon had second thoughts and subsided. All were again forced at gunpoint into the bathroom which, while large, had not been designed for social gatherings of any size.

Frank, angry at Elijah's disrespectful lunge, stuffed him into the bathroom last. "Get your ass in there and wriggle it nice so all them other faggots got somethin' to aim at!" he ordered. This remark was found particularly offensive by the victims, among whom gay rights had not won wide acceptance. Frank ignored their angry comments and piled the loot into a large bag.

But in the meantime the shotgun blast that blew out the light had awakened Mr. George Jones from his nap on the couch in the front room of the empty store, where he was earning his daily bread as a lookout insuring privacy for the players. Jones bolted to his feet, shook his head clear and realized the game was being stuck up. He immediately ran for help; a run which began with his tripping over the couch and crashing through the storefront's plate glass window. The spectacle of a man coming their way through a plate-glass window froze the getaway man and the lookouts in their tracks until Jones had gotten out of range.

Simple of mind but fleet of foot, Jones ran the one block distance to City Hall. There, dashing into the police station he yelled: "They're sticking up the skin game!" to the startled dispatcher.

By the time the resulting various squad cars and police motorcycles arrived with wailing sirens and flashing lights, two of the five robbers had made their getaway. Although hotly pursued by several squad cars in a high-speed chase out of the city and across the causeway to the mainland, they got away and were never caught.

The remaining three, deserted by their colleagues, decided to shoot it out in the dark labyrinth of alleys and tiny back yards that lay behind the store, hoping in the confusion to make their getaway through the wooden fences and scattered trashcans to safety. Many shots were exchanged. Nobody was hit.

Eventually cornered and out of ammunition, Calvin Williams and Edward Jones raised their hands and voices in surrender. They were promptly rushed off to City Hall for their own safety, since the now-freed card players were clamoring for their blood and for their own trousers, in that order.

With commendable presence of mind Frank Satterlee used the final seconds of the shoot-out to climb into a large trash container in a yard behind an adjoining store. He had with him, in addition to his personal armory of pistol and sawed-off shotgun, a bag containing nearly six thousand dollars of the table stakes and an interesting collection of wristwatches, money clips and diamond rings.

The police, with diligence unusual even in such circumstances as these, continued their search of the back alleys, yards, and nearby houses for a full two hours, egged on by the victims, all of whom had retrieved their clothes, their dignity and, fortified with strong drink, now sought the remaining fugitive with the wholehearted energy of outraged decency. Frank stayed put in his trash can, lifting the lid now and then for a quick look around. But the trash can belonged to a back yard, the yard belonged to a house, and the house to a lady who, unable to sleep with all the commotion going on, decided to hang her wash out to dry at four o'clock in the morning. She spotted the lid of the trash can gently closing and alerted a nearby cop. Frank soon found the lid of his temporary shelter lifted. He looked up at the drawn guns of six police officers perfectly happy at the prospect of shooting the fish in this particular barrel.

Slowly, and very carefully, Frank raised his hands. The cops just as carefully removed the pistol from one hand, the shotgun from the other and, when he'd climbed out of the trash can, reached in and retrieved the bag of loot he'd had between his feet. Then, with his hands cuffed behind him, they led this presumably innocent citizen, who was to become my first criminal defendant, off to the squad car.

Chapter 3

Bail of $250,000 meant my guy was on ice. To get out on the street, he'd have to pay the bondsman 10% of it . . . $25,000 he'd never get back even if he got acquitted, which already seemed highly dubious. But he didn't have $25,000. If he did, he would've, as the Public Defender's clientele say, "got hisself a real lawyer!"

The thing about a bail hearing is this; you have to find out everything you can from your client, including his police record and how he was arrested and what they have on him. You have to get all that from your man before you have time to develop what corporate lawyers call a relationship of mutual trust and esteem.

In my case, not much time was needed. Frank Satterlee, who could pass for Bill Cosby's twin brother, was brought into the iron-barred counsel room at the Mays Landing jail and took things right in hand.

"You my lawyer?"

"Yes. I came out to interview you about the bail hearing. It's tomorrow."

"Okay. Now just take it easy," Bill Cosby said with easy confidence. "We gonna get along just fine. What you got to know is they havin' bail hearings tomorrow."

"I just said that."

He ignored the distraction.

"What we got to do is get bail down from two-fifty to maybe fifty. I can get five thousand together, but ain't no way I can come up with $25,000 for no bail bondsman. You got to get it down to fifty grand."

"It won't be easy. They've got some heavy charges against you."

"Yeah, man, but I didn't do it. All that stuff 'bout assault with intent to kill. If I wanted to kill them guys, they'd be dead."

"What happened?"

"They say I tried to kill some dude by hittin' him upside the head with the butt of a sawed off shotgun."

"Did you?"

"No way. That damn fool made a grab for it and I laid the butt longside his head. But no way I was going for to kill him."

"Umm. Frank, you got any police record?"

"Naw. Nothing they gonna know about."

"Nothing they're gonna know about? What? What won't they know about?"

"Nothing. It don't matter. It don't count, cause it got thrown out."

"What got thrown out?"

"They said I killed a guy. But I didn't and it got thrown out."

"You shot a guy?"

"Naw. I whupped him upside the head with the butt of a shotgun. Same's this time. But that ain't what he died from. That's why they threw it out."

"Frank, what did the guy die from?"

"Heart attack. But he lived 32 days after I hit him, 'cause they took him right to the hospital. So they threw it out."

"But Frank, did they throw it out before it went to trial?"

"Nah. On appeal. But they threw it out and these guys won't never know none of that."

"Did you do any time before the appeal got the case thrown out?"

"Yeah, but they won't know about it."

"How much time, Frank?"

"Seventeen years. But it don't count. They threw it out."

"Frank, I think maybe we're going to have problems getting the bail reduced. They'll know all about that record."

"But what about my mother? She's living all alone. Needs me to keep her company."

"After seventeen years, Frank, I expect she can handle it."

Before attending the bail hearing, I thought it prudent to get Frank's view on what is optimistically referred to by defense lawyers as "my client's position." This is always tricky. There are few blessings more helpful to a young defense lawyer than a guilty client who knows the score. They expect to get convicted and slammed with the maximum. If you get them less, they're deeply grateful. If you can actually beat the rap, they spread the word you're a genius, and you get all their repeat business.

On the other hand, few tortures match that of defending a client who insists he's innocent. Even if you get him off so convincingly that the jury sends him flowers and the judge personally apologizes, he'll damn you and the whole system for having charged him in the first place. Give me an honest to God criminal every time.

When I asked Frank if he'd done it, he was refreshingly truthful.

"Yeah, we stuck it up. We'll work out somethin' with the prosecutor. But ain't no way they gonna get me for trying to kill nobody. Anybody I wanna kill, they be dead."

By the time I interviewed Frank I'd read through the file on the case – police reports, witness statements and diagrams. They made me nervous enough to call Chuck McGinty, the piano-playing city editor of the Atlantic City Press. Chuck was a boyhood buddy who had gone from playing cops and robbers to covering their doings. He gave me full access to the morgue, which had all the clippings on the case as the story had originally run.

Whatever their faults, the newspapers know how to tell a story that holds the public's interest. The press believes firmly that the man holding a gun is not an alleged perpetrator and those he sticks up are not witnesses. He is a gunman and they are victims. Easier to follow that way. The story had been a Page One, above-the-fold, 3 photo jackpot for The Press.

After being discovered hiding in the trash can Frank was, reported the Press, promptly handcuffed, led through the crowd to the squad car (Photo on Page One, above the fold), and taken to City Hall. There he was placed in a chair with his hands cuffed behind him while the paperwork began. The Press, ever helpful, ran a photo of Frank, cuffs and chair, also on the front page, and rounded out the trilogy with a third picture of him staring at the camera with strong distaste. This singular honor of three front page photos had never before been granted to any subject of the Press's attention: Not to the President, nor to returning war heroes. Not even the girls arrested at Sonia's whorehouse during the great Christmas raid got that kind of coverage.

The story noted that a sizeable number of the victims had gone to City Hall and there identified Frank as he sat in his chair, adding with uncharacteristic understatement that the identification procedure had to be stopped after "an exchange of words" between the prisoner and the victims threatened to get out of hand, and the police manfully evicted the victims "to protect the prisoner".

I asked Frank if he had any theories as to a good defense. He suggested we follow the line that he had come to play cards and, realizing instantly that he'd be blamed for the stickup because of his record, ran for it. "I ain't gonna testify, you unnerstan'. But if you can get them thinking reasonable doubt, that's one way to do it. Let 'em think I was caught in the stickup just like everybody else."

I made a mental note to bring Frank a cigar. Bill Cosby would have insisted on it.

Chapter 4

I'd been running the Skin Game through the back of my mind while using the vast open spaces at the front to slog my way through the divorces, bankruptcies, and drunk driving cases too small to get sucked in by the dragnets of other law firms.

Ever notice how lawyers in books, movies and on TV zero in on one case at a time? The whole world stops while they do their stuff. Meantime, nobody collects fees, gets paid, or pays the rent. Life should be so good. Twice in my life I've had clients who could pay me enough I could drop everything and take care of that one case. Paradise. But not real life. In real life if you wait to finish one case before taking on three more, you end up selling Big Macs for a living.

The divorce cases were small, but they helped pay the rent. There were always those who paid late, of course, or cried so much I felt guilty charging money to get them freed of their husbands. And then there were those who wanted to pay the fee in more personal currency than money.

You have to be a sport about these things. Just because a girl offers to have sex with you doesn't mean she can't pay cash if necessary. The trick is how to turn down such offers without hurting anybody's feelings – or getting a reputation as one of those holier-than-thou characters nobody wants for a lawyer. Fortunately, I got an early education about the pitfalls of the sex for services deals.

She came in, a good-looking girl nobody I knew would throw out of bed, accompanied by a somewhat overstuffed girl friend who was her confidante. When I'd gotten enough information to know we had grounds for her divorce, it was time to raise the delicate question of the fee.

"That much?" she asked, not really shocked. "Gee, I don't think I can afford it."

"No problem. You've got no kids, and you're already living apart. Keep working, save your money, and come back to see me when you're ready."

A shy smile, a nervous look to her buddy for moral support.

"You know, one of my girl friends went to see Mike Square for her divorce. He didn't charge her anything."

Mike Square was a local shark whose chief claim to fame, aside from being thrown off the bench and temporarily disbarred for fixing traffic tickets while serving as a township judge, was owning a small apartment building in Cherry Hill where he allegedly let apartments only to good – looking single women.

"He didn't charge her anything?" I was skeptical.

"Not a nickel."

"Well, there's your answer! Go see Mike Square. I can't beat his price."

Another nervous glance for support from the girl friend.

"Well, actually it wasn't that he didn't charge her a fee. It's just that she was – you know, nice to him."

"You mean she slept with him to pay for the divorce?"

"Well – yeah !" A shy smile, a hint of naughty blush. "Couldn't we do something like that?"

"Are you bi?"

"What?" The confused look in her eyes was priceless. This wasn't in her script. But she was game, I'll give her that. "No, I'm not bi. I mean, I'll try stuff if it's not too kinky, you know. But couldn't we – "

"That's the problem. My secretary isn't bi either. Besides, she likes getting paid in money. And unless you're willing to spend a few weekends with my landlord and the guys in the electric company, it just won't – "

"Oh, all right," she giggled. "I get the point." Out came the cash, carefully counted and duly receipted.

"I hope I didn't hurt your feelings."

"Oh, that's all right. I thought I'd give it a try." A mischievous glance at her friend. Another giggle. "Actually, she says Mike wasn't that good in bed anyway." Giggles from both as they left.

Mike Square. Not only does he risk losing his license again, but on top of that he ends up with a reputation as a lousy lover! What a putz.

Not every Skin Game played in Atlantic City required dealers, cards, or female flesh. There was white skin and black skin, and everybody got to play the white skin/black skin game, whether they wanted to or not. A few days later I was going through a bankruptcy petition to make sure all the debts were on Schedule A and all the assets on Schedule B. Or is it the other way around? It's hard to stay awake checking a bankruptcy petition. Dottie buzzed to tell me John Wilson wanted to see me.

John Wilson stood high in my book. He was a postal worker, a small quiet black man who sat on the Legal Services Board as a community representative. Never said much, never asked questions, never missed a meeting and never, ever, failed to back me up when the conservative lawyers on the Board suggested I was representing the poor too vigorously. I was no longer running Legal Services, but a friend like that needs no appointment.

He had a son whose juvenile scrapes with the law ended with a Marine Corps recruiter and a ticket to Paris Island. A quiet, respectable citizen was John Wilson.

"Problems, John?" I expected to hear the Marine Corps had put return postage on his son.

Tears welled up in his eyes. "It's kinda embarrassing." He rubbed his forehead to avoid looking at me. "It's the Post Office."

"What happened?"

"They've put in the paperwork to fire me."

Some guys can say they're getting fired and you don't blink. John wasn't one of them. I blinked. Twice.

"What the hell for?"

"Well," he choked up, then edged into it, "there's one of them little fire alarm boxes on the staircase – the kind with a little glass door you break with that tiny hammer that hangs on a chain? Somebody broke it and set off the alarm. They say it was me."

"They're blaming you?" I was flabbergasted.

He nodded glumly.

"That's bullshit! How'd they come up with that?"

He rubbed his forehead again, ran his hand over the top of his head, put both hands on his knees, then had another try at his forehead.

"I told them."

When I got over the shock, I had John tell me what they said. What they asked and what he answered.

When you think of it, it's funny. C'mon, be honest. Haven't you ever felt the urge to push the red button just to see what happens? Sure it's illegal and a pain in the ass for fireman. And like the politicians say, what happens if instead of snoozing or playing cards they're needed to save the old ladies in the nursing home ? Still, think of all the time they waste washing fire trucks. Maybe false alarms keep them on their toes. Who knows?

The good news was they hadn't asked the one question that mattered. Once John 'fessed up to ringing the alarm, they figured they'd caught him in the woodpile, and now was their chance to improve the white/black ratio in the post office by a kangaroo court and a quick hanging.

"John, how bad was the smell of smoke?"

"Wha? There wasn't no . . .

"Dammit, John. Think! How bad was the smell of smoke?"

"But there wasn't no . . . oh! OH! Yeah! Yeah, I thought I smelled smoke!" His eyes lit up like a little kid at Christmas. "You know, I think I really did smell smoke. But they never asked me that! They never asked *why* I rang that alarm!" The smile on his face was a wonder to see.

"Right. They *assumed* you were doing something wrong, because you probably looked guilty as hell. Sure did when you came in here."

John wasn't the first black worker in the Atlantic City Post Office. The first was in the late 40's. I knew that because my deaf old Aunt Mary, who read fortunes in her apartment over the liquor store at Indiana and Atlantic and was almost as blind as she was deaf, shot the poor bastard in the foot when he tried to deliver her mail. "I thought he was a burglar!" she protested. "How was I supposed to know they were hiring niggers?" Aunt Mary was burdened with more than deafness, bad eyes, and a strong dose of bigotry. She was a fortuneteller, and she'd had an inkling that something bad was coming her way. All that was coming her way was Uncle Jule's pension check from the Spanish-American War, and the guy that delivered it got shot in the foot for his efforts.

But however many black workers the Post Office had, none had ever been Postmaster, or Assistant Postmaster, or anything higher than mail handler until John Wilson came along. In a just world, he would have risen to be Postmaster himself – a fact fully understood by the white Postmaster, the white Assistant Postmaster, and the white officials of the Postal Worker's Union, all of whom had spent years making damn sure no black got promoted. Aunt Mary was a joke compared to the damage those guys did.

So I dictated a letter to the Postmaster and, no pun intended, blackmailed the son of a bitch. With John sitting there grinning like a kid let loose from school, I informed the Postmaster that my client had smelled smoke, acted promptly by punching the fire alarm, and unless he was reinstated immediately with full pay, an apology, and all charges dismissed and purged from his file, there'd be hell to pay, including a cluster of civil rights suits filed against the government, the union that refused to defend John, and the Postmaster personally. It took a few weeks, but it worked. Try proving that somebody *didn't* think they smelled smoke.

I've never since been able to pass a fire alarm without a grin.

Chapter 5

A call to the Clerk's office alerted me to the fact that the prosecution of the Skin Game stick-up had been placed in the dubious care of Billy O'Hara, known as "Squeaks" because of his high-pitched voice and freshly-scrubbed appearance. Squeaks had worked for me in Legal Services where under the rules of court he could try cases while he sweated out the results of his bar exams. At 32, he still lived at home with his mother, went to church every Sunday, and never, never smoked, drank, gambled, cursed or went out with women loose or otherwise. His cheeks were always pink, his shoes gleamingly polished, his shirt neatly pressed, his hair, already thinning, neatly combed. In court he had an unfortunate tendency to stammer when unsure of his case. This in turn made him nervous enough to blush, which always made him break out into a high-pitched giggle. His adversaries learned to listen for the first stammer, and to bore in on the weak spot in his cases, guided by the arrival of the blush and homing in when they got to the giggle.

He flunked the bar exam on his first try, took it again six months later, flunked again, and again and again.

After his fourth flunk several well-meaning veterans of the Bar pointed out that spending the evening before the exam in meaningful social intercourse with a young lady might help him relax. One lawyer went so far as to set up a free session for Squeaks with an attractive client of his known for her professional ability to help distressed young men relax in charmingly direct ways. Squeaks tried to stammer out a "no thanks" but got caught in a high-pitched nervous giggle, blushed for a half-hour, and flunked the Bar exam four more times before passing on his eighth try.

Squeaks believed what his mother taught him about the poor being sinfully lazy. He believed landlords were always right and justified in their treatment of tenants. He believed the finance company had every right in the world to repossess the furniture when the deadbeats didn't pay. If there were exorbitant interest rates and fuzzy fine print on some of the contracts the poor signed, he asked himself, why didn't they just refuse to sign them? He wasn't happy in Legal Services, although after a few cases he learned to speak as slowly as possible, which helped him get by in court except when the pressure built.

When Squeaks finally passed the Bar he made a beeline for a job with the county prosecutor, where he was carefully assigned only to cases in which there were at least four eye-witnesses, the defendant was arrested with the loot on him, and the judge was a sure bet.

Frank's case was made to order for Squeaks. There never was a friendlier judge for a prosecutor to draw than Vinnie Raffaelli, who caught the case at the bail hearing and stayed with it all through the trial.

Raffaelli was a boring, buck-toothed, bug-eyed, bald-headed son of a bitch who prided himself on running fair trials. Which he did, except for the occasional outbreak of hangman's itch, an occupational disease of former prosecutors who make it to the bench. But after a conviction, Vinnie believed prisoners needed long, serious time to reflect on their mistakes. It never occurred to him that "Give 'em a fair trial and then hang 'em." was supposed to be a joke.

Raffaelli was highly predictable on bail. If the case made the front page within the past two months bail was high. If it never made the paper at all, you could sign yourself out. An unlucky mother of seven kids, one of whom had been accepted to college, starred in a news feature about how tough it was to make it on welfare. She told a not-too-bright reporter she'd been cleaning houses on the side for cash to supplement the welfare check. The day after the paper hit the street with her name in plain print she was indicted for welfare fraud. Raffaelli held her on $200,000, insisting that she couldn't be trusted to stick around for the trial. I pointed out she'd been born here, all of her kids were born here, and all of them had perfect attendance records at school. But Raffaelli wasn't about to look soft on welfare fraud – not with his re-appointment coming up. It took me two full days of work on appeal to get her cut loose.

Unfortunately for Frank Satterlee, his case was the stuff news reporters dream about. It had movie rights written all over it. A gang of heavies from Newark down here in easy-going Atlantic City sticking up a card game, window-busting, guns everywhere, twenty-two grown men forced to strip and crowd into a bathroom, a big shoot-out, a high speed car chase in which two of the five got away, an arrest at four in the morning on the hottest night action corner in town complete with reporters and photographers. We were up against three-inch headlines and above-the-fold photographs of my guy being led away in handcuffs, and a long, juicy indictment topped off with six counts of assault with intent to kill police officers.

I had no hope of a bail reduction. Frank was more optimistic. As he explained with the patience of an expert taking a rookie under his wing, the delicate protocol of jail reservations had gotten badly out of hand. The State was in the habit of parking state prisoners in the county jails instead of paying for new state prisons. This allowed the State Attorney General to hold news conferences announcing the arrests of big time criminals. It let the State Senators and State Assemblymen pass laws setting stiff mandatory jail sentences without having to raise taxes to build the prisons. On the other hand, the county politicians refused to raise county taxes to build county jails to handle the prisoners dumped on them by the State. The resulting attempts to stuff five hundred prisoners into a jail built for two hundred had finally convinced even our right wing federal district court judge that he'd have to order a new jail built unless the state judges started popping loose all prisoners who'd refrained from killing anybody in the past year. In effect, the political-judicial gridlock made jail space harder to get than tickets to the Superbowl.

Frank watched the proceedings at the bail hearing with the cool eye of experience and the confidence born of a professional's inside assessment of the jail's capacity and the intricacies of federal, state and local tax burdens. It occurred to me the prison population could probably teach college professors a thing or two about this arcane area of political science.

"Not bad, Frank," I commented, hearing the bail drop to one fifty.

"Ain't good either. Coulda got it down to a hunnerd, I ain't got no fifteen thousand. We gotta try again, later on, jail gets mo' crowded."

"Give my love to your mother, Frank."

Chapter 6

Although it seemed a hopeless case, there was always a chance of a lucky break. Witnesses don't always show up for the trial, particularly witnesses like these twenty-two hard cases, some of whom had warrants out for their own arrests. Several of them would probably be in jail themselves by the time the trial came around.

Admittedly there were the police officer witnesses to contend with. But even there the luck of the draw might go our way. The police department was having its own troubles. At the moment, the odds of any given police officer being unavailable for trial were almost even. Three of the five City Commissioners and a full thirty-seven percent of the police force were under indictment, courtesy of a misunderstanding between the local politicians and their colleagues from North Jersey, which resulted in a burst of anti-corruption investigations of the city by the state government.

State investigators soon learned that finding corruption in Atlantic City was easier than finding your ass using both hands. State undercover cops set up a dummy fencing operation in an old garage. They put the word out on the street that they were open for business. Soon hidden cameras were filming a constant stream of crooks bringing in their loot to sell for cash, all unaware of their starring roles in the next session of the grand jury.

Happy with their haul, the state police were about to close up shop when a city motorcycle cop in full uniform and on his hog drove into the garage. After initial small talk it became clear the motorcycle cop knew they were buying stolen goods. The state undercover guys figured their cover was blown. They were about to show their credentials to the motorcycle cop when it finally dawned on them that he wasn't there to investigate the fencing operation. He was there to sell his motorcycle. The resulting film of the fully-uniformed cop walking away from the city's Harley Davidson stuffing the cash into his pocket with a satisfied grin had the grand jury in tears of laughter. When the news broke, the Motorcycle Division was less concerned with the sale than with the outrageously low price for which their colleague sold his bike.

There were the cops who stole the copper pipes from vacant houses, the usual cops who shook down the hookers, and then, of course, there was the Great Undertakers War.

I liked the Undertakers War. It showed the free enterprise system in full swing. The deal was that if you died poor – and murder victims seldom have estate lawyers – the state coughed up money for your funeral. Two undertakers enjoyed most of the business on the Northside, which is where black folk have the monopoly on poverty and murders. Which undertaker planted your remains depended on which cop found your body – each cop having a private arrangement with his undertaker of choice.

All worked well until private ambulance companies sprang up to replace the non-profit volunteers that once carried you free to the hospital. Under the new system, a private, profit-making ambulance company that carried you to the hospital got paid – either by your insurance company or, if you were poor, by the state. This brought a new and energetic element into the affair, as the several ambulance companies made their private arrangements with the cops.

It soon became clear that whether a victim was sent to the hospital or the undertaker depended less on whether he was still breathing than on which cop found him. Races soon developed, in which one radio report could result in a half-dozen squad cars, two ambulances, and two hearses surrounding a victim. In short order this led to sharp words, then fisticuffs. When a reporter chanced upon a ten-man brawl between cops, undertakers, and ambulance drivers while the victim lay moaning in the street, the resulting story led to a lively meeting at City Hall in which both undertakers, both ambulance companies, and six cops were summoned to the Chief's office. There, amidst bellowing rage and threats of imprisonment and loss of pensions and the use of physical force, a *detente cordiale* was hammered out which allocated the victims according to the voting ward in which they fell. The ambulance driver would henceforth take all bodies, dead or alive, to the hospital, with a gentleman's understanding that the undertaker for that ward would get any planting work subsequently needed.

Given all that, I had reason to hope we could limit the vexing problem of having police officers testify against Frank as eyewitnesses to the shootout at the Skin Game. I looked over the names of the police officers in hopes of finding new headaches for the prosecutor, and hit paydirt immediately. Of the four we had to contend with, two were alumni of the vice squad, reassigned pending investigations as to whether they were overly connected with the municipal judge, who, it was rumored, had his own string of hookers and jollied the vice squad into rounding up the competition whenever a convention hit town. These two in particular had featured prominently in the street rumors as being on the Judge's payroll. Of the remaining two cops, one was unlikely to have been sober at the time of the arrests, and even more unlikely to be sober at the trial.

Frank Satterlee's luck ran out, however, when we reached Jack Jenner. Jack and I went through grade school and high school together. He'd gone on the force and spent the next ten years as a motorcycle cop too honest to get promoted. Being honest, he was usually assigned to the black neighborhoods where honest law enforcement wouldn't get in the way of the Boardwalk and Pacific Avenue trade. After ten years as a white cop policing black neighborhoods, he had a fully developed racist and right-wing set of beliefs. With his views, however, had come enough experience to know one black person from another, even in dim light and under stress. "Ya gotta know the good niggers from the bad niggers," he said, and prided himself on being able to do just that. The blacks cordially hated him, but in his career not a single civil rights complaint was ever filed against him, nor did a single defendant ever get off on the basis of mistaken identification; a record unique in a town where white cops routinely considered any nearby blacks as suspects, and were as prone to lock up the minister as the thief.

Jack would be at the trial. He would be stone cold sober. He would testify. And if he identified Frank Satterlee, nobody would have the slightest doubt that Frank Satterlee was the man with the shotgun.

I called Jack and asked him if he was able to identify Frank Satterlee.

"Yeah. I was the guy that hauled him outta the trash can."

"Jack, he says he only came to play cards, blew his cool, grabbed the stuff and tried to run away."

"He's telling you he didn't do the stickup?"

"Sort of."

"Well, I dunno whether he was there to stick the game up or not."

"So your testimony will be that you only saw him in the trashcan?"

"Nope. My testimony is that when I got up the alley the stickup was over, and guys were running in all directions. But I'm gonna also testify that I saw that motherfucker running down the alley with the guns and the bag of loot, told him to stop, and that the son of a bitch took five shots at me while I was looking right at him. That's how come I kept looking for him for the next two hours, and that's how come I recognized the scumbag when I got him."

"Ouch."

"Yeah. Well, counselor, you get this fucker off, you'll be the busiest lawyer in town after that."

"I gotta try, Jack."

"Yeah, I know. No hard feelings. But don't lose too much sleep when the jury says guilty without leaving the box. Didja know he did seventeen years in Pennsylvania?"

"What for?"

"Same thing as here. Hit a guy in the head with a shotgun butt. Guy went into the hospital and died, but not for a month or two after the hit, so your guy kept appealing until he finally made it."

"Hmm. Tell me Jack, did he give you any grief when you took him in?"

"Ya know, that's the damndest thing. The guy was a perfect gentleman. Here he tries to blow my fuckin' head off, but when I got him into the Hall, he was nice as pie. Even asked me if I was okay after the shootin.'"

"Yeah. He loves his mother too."

"Maybe the guy just wants to go back to prison. Seventeen years inside, ya know, they get used to it. Get so they can't make it on the outside."

"Thanks Jack. I'll keep that in mind."

It was obviously time to come up with a trial strategy. This I did one night while watching a movie about a skier trying to outrun an avalanche. No form, no finesse. Just go with whatever works and don't look back. I started out with a guilty client; a benefit few lawyers have. Frank made no bones about doing the stick-up. He didn't agree with the attempted murder charge on Elijah Morton, but aside from that felt the charges of assault with intent to kill police officers could only enhance his reputation in prison.

The fly in the ointment was that his two co-defendants refused to plea.

There are cases you try, and cases you plea. Without a plea bargain, Frank faced about 40 years with no parole. He was willing to deal. All he wanted was the shortest sentence, which he had calculated at 7 to 10, although he figured more realistically on a 12 to 20 with time off for good behavior, getting him out on the street again in 7 years.

Squeaks the prosecutor was willing to deal but, with the Atlantic City Police Department on his ass, was under orders not to deal unless all three pleaded. Calvin Williams wouldn't deal at all, and Eddie Jones, who had never actually entered the stickup room and had hopes for his defense, wanted to hold out for 3 to 5 with parole in 18 months. This neither Squeaks nor Judge Raffaelli would go for.

These concerns did not worry Frank unduly. As he saw it, we were just going through the motions. Squeaks knew we wanted to deal, and Raffaelli knew we wanted to deal. And Raffaelli had enough of the old Prosecutor in him to lighten up on Frank when we got to sentencing day, if only as a way to stick it to the other two for not pleading.

"Don' worry, my man. Them guys are gonna plea before it's over."

We'll go along with the trial and maybe get lucky. If they plea, we get what we want and if they don't, jury says guilty, I figure we still gonna get the same sentence. Nobody got hurt and they ain't gonna have jail room, all them guys sellin' dope to kids."

So we had a free ride. Still, I was getting paid to try a case. If I could win, a hardened criminal would be free to continue to prey on other hardened criminals. And, as Jack Jenner said, if I could get this motherfucker off I had it made!

For this, I needed a trial strategy. Frank had no moral scruples about testifying. He was perfectly willing to go on the witness stand and swear he was home in bed when it all happened. But he saw my point about getting slammed with perjury charges to add to his inevitable prison sentence, and agreed the risk was unacceptable. I had no worries about a defendant eager to bare his soul and tell all.

Given all that, the trial strategy was fairly obvious. When you have no alibi, a defendant who can't testify, and twenty or thirty eyewitnesses swearing he was the man, your best hope is to cross examine every one of them, dragging in as many red herrings as you can to create whatever reasonable doubt can be milked out of the inevitable discrepancies between the memories of thirty different witnesses.

In Frank's case, this meant using my questions to insinuate that: (a) Frank was an innocent stranger who stopped by to join a card game he'd heard about and got caught in and blamed for the stick-up precisely because he was a stranger; (b) realizing this, he'd panicked and run, ducking into a trash can; (c) on his way picking up the shotgun, pistol, and loot dropped by one of the real robbers in his haste to get away; and (d) that the card game was under corrupt police protection, which made it imperative that the police solve the crime, nailing Frank as the perfect scapegoat.

That's a lot of innuendo. But you can do a lot with sneaky questions. I had almost 30 prospective witnesses to cross examine. Worth a try. And, as Frank noted, "Relax. We jes' along fo the ride."

However, it'd be nice to win, if only to watch how many shades of purple Raffaelli would turn when the verdict came in.

Chapter 7

While I was wrapped up in Frank's problems and those of various divorcees, bankrupts, and drunk drivers, Christmas snuck up on me. I heard a strange sound one afternoon. Turned out to be the Salvation Army Santa Claus on the avenue, hustling shoppers for loose change.

The Law, as musty old scholars say, is a conservative force in society. How right they are. Five hundred years ago some King took the royal court hunting at Christmas, so five hundred years later nobody tries criminal cases from the middle of December until the middle of January. When the jail got crowded enough I got Frank's bail dropped to $25,000. Frank paid the bondsman the necessary $2,500 and went home to spend the holidays with his dear old mother.

Christmas, in the days before the casinos arrived and hired their own Santa Clauses on the theory that any loose change rightfully belonged in their slot machines, was a dreary time in Atlantic City. The temperature dropped, the winds picked up, the poor bought extra tinsel to keep themselves warm, and such conventions as still came to town dried up for a month. It was the week before Christmas, and time for the annual raid on Sonia's whorehouse.

When I tell the story about Sonia's, I have to tell about Mary the nearsighted hooker. And to appreciate Mary the nearsighted hooker you have to know how I came to represent most of the really good looking independent hookers in town. And for that I have to tell you about Cindy, one of the last clients I handled at the Legal Services office before I left to open my own shop.

Cindy was 14 when she ran away from home, a big-boned, plain looking farm girl whose youth was her main asset in the looks department. She wasn't exactly retarded, but she was as slow as you can get and not block traffic. Her saving grace was that there wasn't a mean thought in her head. Damn few thoughts at all, but such as she had were good-natured and kind.

I don't know why she ran away from home. By the time she came into my office that part was ancient history. She'd landed in Atlantic City living with a sleazeball who ran a four booth luncheonette and deli in the Inlet section of town. If you were running away from home the north Inlet was as far as you could go without a boat. Originally filled with spacious summer houses that had wide porches and plenty of bedrooms for the servants, it had slipped from Wasp to lace-curtain Irish to shanty Irish and was halfway to Black on its way to Hispanic and finally Asian, who'd start up enough sushi bars and dry cleaners to tempt the Wasps to move back in.

Cindy got pregnant and had a baby girl. The sleazeball celebrated fatherhood by developing a nose for white powder of the sort the law optimistically calls a "controlled" dangerous substance, which is about as effectively controlled as seagull shit. Money fights followed. She tried leaving, but the sleazeball's manly pride dictated that he keep the baby. You'd be amazed at what people use to keep score. Money, cars, television sets, kids. So long as you've got something to prove you won.

So she stayed. He started whining about expenses, and how they could make a fast hundred bucks if she'd sleep with his buddy who had the hots for her. She wasn't into that sort of thing, but it was a tossup who cried louder, him or the hungry baby. So she went along with it. The buddy was an undercover cop who busted her for prostitution. When court came up, sleazeball turned lawyer and advised her if she fought it and was found guilty the judge would give her 30 days, whereas if she plead guilty and promised she wouldn't do it again she'd only get a fine. She did what he said and pleaded guilty. When they got home sleazeball kicked her out and kept the baby on the grounds that no court would make him give it up because as an admitted prostitute she was an unfit mother.

She drifted into the life for real, swinging her bag up and down Pacific Avenue, negotiating with visiting heroes through rolled down car windows. "Negotiating" is probably the wrong word. Cindy's mental hardware wasn't fast enough for addition, subtraction, or remembering different prices for different services. She was the Dollar store of hookerdom. Every item priced the same. And she made a living. Pacific Avenue is the main street for conventioneers in Atlantic City. They're usually in good supply, and when they aren't, the locals can always be counted on to drive by and do a little business. Hookers are another variation of the Atlantic City skin game – the more you pay, the more skin you see.

Pacific Avenue is a long street served by jitneys, which are 13-passenger buses that whiz you uptown and down from Convention Hall to hotels to show bars and back again. On any given night, a jitney driver zips along Pacific Avenue 12 or 15 times. It's impossible for a jitney driver not to recognize the hookers working the street. When one of them fell in love with Cindy, he had no illusions about how she earned her living.

But love conquers all. He agreed to forget the past; she agreed to give up the life and go straight. They got married, the hooker and the jitney driver, and proceeded to live happily ever after. Except that Cindy, no longer able to have children and determined to keep her word about no more turning tricks, had no chance of landing a straight job. Even the Dollar store wants its workers smart enough to keep the dollar when they change a ten dollar bill. Without a job, and with her husband driving the jitney extra shifts to support them, Cindy had a lot of time with nothing to do but pine for her absent baby girl. Which eventually led her to my office, hoping against hope that I could find a way to get her baby back.

Fools rush in where angels fear to tread, which about describes a young lawyer taking on the job of persuading a judge to restore custody of a little girl to a convicted prostitute. But I put my investigator, 75-year-old "First Count" Collins, on the job. First Count, a small, spry, café au lait fashion plate of a man who billed himself as "the world's best colored pool player", was also known as "Baby." When I asked about his nicknames, he said he'd won the "Baby" from his first girlfriend, and all his girlfriends since had liked it. Even at 75, he was the smoothest ladies's man in town.

"Now, that 'First Count' name," he said, "that's 'cause when I do business, I always make sure I'm the first one to count the money. I got that from my daddy. I remember him tellin' me when I was a young boy. Said it don't matter who your partner is, long's you get first count of the money!" Plenty of business schools can't teach it that well.

First Count came through in style. Within days he tracked down the sleazeball, who'd moved to Pleasantville over on the mainland. He was living in a dilapidated house and was under surveillance by the police for suspected drug dealing. The little girl, now four years old, was filthy, dressed in rags, and playing in a yard full of trash, including the occasional hypodermic needle. I sent First Count out again with a camera.

It was an easy win. The judge, a distinguished and honest lawyer who'd been appointed by the corrupt political machine as a stick-on deodorant in hopes his good name would let them win one more election, took one look at the pictures, read the pleadings, and signed a court order within five minutes. The sleazeball didn't even try fighting it.

I gave full credit to First Count, but Cindy, who came back a week later with a basket of fruit and a scrubbed, smiling, immaculately dressed little girl, convinced herself I was the greatest legal genius of all time. She raved about me to all her closest friends. Who, of course, were hookers. Within a few weeks of opening my office, my secretary began giving me strange looks as she opened new case files on a succession of beautiful young women who'd been charged with solicitation for prostitution.

"We should make up a rubber stamp: 'Referred by Cindy'," she said. "Who the hell's Cindy?"

"Just a good friend."

"Yeah! Right!" Of such misunderstandings are sullied reputations made. "Well, your good friend just sent in another hooker. Want her now?"

"Could you rephrase that?"

I liked Mary from the minute I met her.

"Cindy said you're the best, and God knows I need the best. She said pay you whatever you ask, 'cause you're worth it."

What's not to like in a client like that?

Mary's problem was that she was nearsighted. Without glasses, she couldn't see her own feet. Or anybody else's. She'd been working Red Morgan's bar, and followed up on an interested conventioneer, only to find too late he was an undercover cop.

"How'd they catch you?"

"Oh, God, I'm so stupid! The guy was wearing cop shoes! Only without my glasses I couldn't see them, and what girl's gonna wear glasses in my line of work? Can you get me off?"

I called my rabbi, Sam Goldstein, for advice. Sam was admitted to the Bar the year Roosevelt beat Alf Landon, and what he didn't know about practicing law in Atlantic City wasn't worth knowing. He loved telling stories more than I do. If you were willing to listen, you could learn more in five minutes from Sam than from a year in the average law school.

"Consorting with people with a bad reputation. Fifty bucks," he said.

"Put that in English, Sam."

"Show up in Municipal Court and plead her not guilty. When she's found guilty, she'll get thirty days. You post a $500 bond and appeal that."

"You don't think I can win in Municipal Court?"

"Not with hookers." Sam's voice became pious and solemn, "I'm sure there's not an ounce of truth in it, you understand" Sam paused and cleared his throat, "But I've heard it said the Judge has his own string of 'em. Whenever a convention hits town he has the cops arrest the independents. He gives them 30 days to keep them from competing with his girls. Can't possibly be true," I could see his tongue in his cheek right over the telephone, "but if I was you I'd have the appeal papers ready before you walk into his courtroom. The minute he sentences her, go across the street to the State Court. File the appeal papers and ask for bail. They always grant that. She'll be out in a coupla hours. When they get around to hearing the appeal, plea bargain with the prosecutor. Get the charge downgraded to consorting with people with a bad reputation and . . ."

"That's an offense? Hanging out with people with a bad reputation?"

"It's still on the books. You plea her guilty to that, it's a fifty-dollar fine and she walks. The main thing is keeping her working by filing that appeal right away. That's how you earn your fee." It worked like a charm. Mary thought it was great. So did the other hookers I helped stay afloat in the rocky stream of commerce.

When they wanted to consort with a person of bad reputation and good money, the hookers towed their catch to Sonia's whorehouse. Sonia's, like most of Atlantic City, was living on the faded glory and peeling paint of happier days. Sonia's own happy days stretched back to 1910, when the Roosevelt in politics was Teddy and the Boardwalk sparkled with presidents, opera stars, and brand new millionaires from Chicago. She'd come to town a luscious 17-year-old with a portly old gentleman who was not her uncle, and never left. By the Roaring Twenties she had customers arriving in private railroad cars, and by the Thirties had her own establishment; the sort of place to which the best men brought their sons for their 21st birthdays.

One old-timer told me, with longing in his eyes, what it was like in the days when Sonia treated her girls to a day at the races – a parade of twenty or so beautiful girls dressed to perfection, strolling across Columbus Plaza to the train station on a fine spring day for the excursion special to Delaware Park, a small squad of porters following with picnic baskets and champagne.

Atlantic City was a big rest and recreation town during World War II. Some of the big hotels converted to convalescent hospitals. Sonia did her patriotic duty. She made sure none of the boys in uniform got robbed or overcharged. Guys with arms or legs missing were as welcome at Sonia's as anyone else, and their champagne was on the house. Any soldier too drunk to walk was sent home in a taxicab.

After the war and through the Fifties the big acts were always in town – Frank Sinatra, Dean Martin and Jerry Lewis at the 500 Club, Slappy White opening for Sammy Davis, Jr. at the Club Harlem on Kentucky Avenue near Sammy's mother's place, Grace's Belmont Inn. But the Sixties brought trouble, in the form of the passenger jet – the great silver birds that kidnaped the big-spending winter conventions and flew away with them to Vegas, San Juan – wherever the sun kept shining and you could play golf in December and February and gamble in style. Salt water taffy and shivering strolls on the Boardwalk suddenly lost their appeal.

Each winter fewer hookers came back for the convention season. The champagne drinking conventions headed elsewhere. In their place came the beer drinkers of the American Legion, the Elks, the Policemen's Benevolent Association, the school teachers, and Japanese biologists whose convention planners were still working from pre-war travel magazine ads. In '64 the Democrats came to town to nominate Lyndon Johnson, but all the national press wrote about was Atlantic City's crummy hotels, sleazy bars, and lousy restaurants. They made you think every delegate had been issued a souvenir cockroach.

Sonia doggedly held on. There was still enough business to keep a half-dozen good-looking girls reasonably busy, and Sonia was enough of a businesswoman to cut expenses. Instead of live-in girls on the payroll, she rented rooms to the girls as independent contractors. Only the best girls, but they had to bring their own customers. Conventioneers no longer came and picked out their favorites from a bevy of available beauties. They headed for the bars where the girls had arrangements with the bartenders so they could sip tea in highball glasses and wait for the fish.

When the classy girls who once graced Sonia's started working the bars, the bar hookers, sliding down the survival chain, started working the streets. Competition on the street soon got fierce. The streetwalkers walked up to cars, rapped on the windows, even took to opening their blouses to show the merchandise. This was part hustling, part truth-in-advertising. Transvestites were becoming serious competition. It wasn't long before horny johns assumed every woman on Pacific Avenue was a hooker – which didn't sit well with nurses coming off the night shift at the hospital. Came the night one of the hookers stopped a bigshot businessman from New York who was walking with his wife and announced she could do more for him than his Mrs. Unfortunately, the Mrs. lacked that broad-minded, bawdy humor so helpful when dealing with such moments. Even more unfortunately, she happened to be a corporate lawyer heavily connected to the convention industry.

So hell was raised, reforms were demanded, and the cops had to bust hookers. But how to do that without hurting business?

A deal was worked out. To satisfy the politicians, the cops would bust hookers in a few well-publicized raids. But to make sure no desperately needed convention business was lost, the raids would be staged just before Christmas when nobody was in town. Sonia, whose place had featured in similar show raids back in the 30's, was willing to go along in exchange for getting the competition off the streets, and for the free advertising. And the press, happy to have a juicy sex headline during a slow news time, was willing to give the cops all the ink they wanted.

It worked perfectly. The press covered the raids, the cops got letters of commendation in their personnel files, the politicians got credit for doing something about crime, the hookers got light bail and, when their cases came up weeks later, got off with token fines. It worked so well they repeated it the next year, and the next. Thus was born the tradition of the annual Christmas raid on Sonia's whorehouse. It soon became as much a part of the holiday season as the high school Thanksgiving Day game and indicting the Mayor.

"Donovan, you've gotta help me!" Mary the nearsighted hooker called me in mid-afternoon of Christmas Eve.

"Sonia's?" I'd just come back from lunch, where the Boardwalk version of the bush telegraph was up to date with the news. Putting the proverbial two and two together, I was reasonably sure Mary had been caught in the raid.

"Yeah. What a drag! It's okay, though. I made bail. But they stole Sonia's shoebox! You gotta help her!"

The Irish call it the sugarbowl, the Poles call it the stash, the Jews call it the pishka. What we all mean is the cookie jar – the place you hide the cash you'll need on that rainy day when the IRS or an angry spouse grabs your bank account. With Sonia it was "The Shoe Box", depository of every dollar she'd squirreled away over the fat years and the lean. Nobody knew how much was in it. I'd once lazed through a lunch with two old-timers who spent the hour craftily trying to figure it out, like kids guessing how many jelly beans were in the great big jar. Nobody knew. But it was a lot, and whether a lot or a little, it was all she had.

The raid was shabby in the extreme. Sonia, trying to make the best of hard times, had taken to renting the three top-floor rooms to more or less permanent boarders. In one of those the police had installed a brand new, waiting-for-the-next-class-at-the-police-academy recruit.

It occurs to me that some readers may have no acquaintance with hookers, and others might not know any cops. Even those who move in either or both circles socially may, in these days of escort services and massage parlors, never have actually visited an old-fashioned whorehouse. Some background may help. Those sinners familiar with such matters can skip lightly over the next passages, provided you say three Hail Mary's and make a good act of contrition as you go.

Busting hookers is, by definition, an up-close and personal police activity. You can't do it by CIA satellite, by remote TV cameras, or by infra-red. Much of the hooker's marketing is a matter of inflection, suggestion, great privacy, and serious ambiguity. Consider, for example, the following typical exchange between, say, Brandy (or Samantha, or Crystal) and John:

> BRANDY: "Hi, there! Got a match?"
> JOHN: "For somebody as good lookin' as you? Sure!"

BRANDY: "Thanks"

JOHN: (Nods his head.)

BRANDY: (Sits silently, giving John slow, sensuous, inviting looks, none of which are any good to the prosecution in court.)

JOHN "So what's a guy do for fun around here?"

BRANDY: (Smiles knowingly) "Depends what you like."

JOHN: "I like it all!"

BRANDY: (Sexily, leaning forward): "Yeah, well lots of guys do."

You see the problem. She's already got him breathing heavy and not an incriminating word's been said. If John's a plainclothes cop, he can't blurt out "How much for sex?" That's what defense lawyers call "entrapment!" complete with the exclamation point and a look of shock. "Your Honor, this innocent young virgin would never have committed this naughty act had not the police officer himself suggested she sell her body for sex. Oh, the shame of it!" But somebody's got to go first, which means either the John asks the straightforward question, or the hooker works on him until he does.

Fortunately for the cops, many johns are nervous, sweating, shaking, out of their element, and worried about what happens if somebody who knows them sees them at this most delicate of moments. Sometimes the hooker has to take the lead to get things moving. This, eventually, gets her busted, which permanently engraves on her memory the face of the S.O.B. that arrested her. Any hooker in the life more than two weeks can draw you a rogue's gallery of every cop on the vice squad. They pass around descriptions among the sisterhood.

In a sort of arms race, the vice squad guys bring in their buddies from traffic patrol. The girls learn to recognize them. The cops escalate and bring in cops from nearby small towns. The word spreads through the network: "Be careful about the tall, skinny guy with sideburns. He's a cop."

Until, at last, the cops hire a few new rookies. New faces, impossible for the girls to recognize. Of course, rookies make serious mistakes –

like letting their coats fall open and their guns show, always a tip-off to a reasonably observant hooker. But that's what rookies are used for. Find a guy who just got on the force, and next day he's bragging about the hookers he busted last night.

And that's what Mrs. Hengleman's boy Harold was used for. Freshly sworn in and set up as a resident snoop at Sonia's, Hengleman was ordered to gather evidence of that most horrible of crimes, sex in a private place between two eagerly consenting adults.

Following Rabbi Sam's advice, I wanted Sonia's case tried as soon as possible, before the dolt wised up to the proper way to frame, lie, and look sincere when testifying in court. Applying the highly scrutable logic of the Trial Court Administrator's (known to his intimates as "the TCA") scheduling system, and with only a little cheating as coached by Sam, I got Sonia's case put at the head of the list when court resumed in January. It's easier than it sounds. The TCA makes you fill out a form and give your best estimate of the trial time needed. Since the TCA's job performance . . . and that of the judges . . . is measured by how many cases go through the sluices, half-day cases get tried first. If you want delay, you insist the case will take months. If you want things to zip along, you put down a half-day. I put down a half-day and the case floated to the top like bubbles in the bathtub.

According to the police reports, rookie Hengleman had seen every transaction; heard every word, and saw the money change hands before the hookers and their johns went into the bedrooms on the floor below his room. Mary insisted there was no way he could have seen or heard what he claimed; not from the third floor front. To get the facts straight, I arranged to meet her at Sonia's. It wasn't on my usual trek around town, but no good lawyer should avoid visiting a whorehouse when duty requires.

Atlantic City being built on a big sandbar, the local idea of a basement is what other folks think of as the first floor. To get to the first floor of the part you live in, you climb the outside steps, walk across the porch, and ring the bell. Eventually Sonia let us into her home. I looked around with an appreciative eye at this romantic, mysterious, fabled resort of sex for sale. First, of course, I had to look at Sonia, whose 76 year-old sore feet in frayed slippers supported the accumulated pounds, wrinkles, arthritic joints and aches of hard years, topped by a suspicious face of the kind the Russians stationed in Moscow hotel corridors to watch tourists for the KGB. After the introductions, which converted me from a mid-afternoon john to a semi-accepted ally, we went upstairs to see what the cop could have seen or not seen.

I asked what kind of boarder Hengleman had been. Whatever gracious turn of genteel phrase Sonia may have acquired in her early days had, like the weatherbeaten paint, long since peeled off.

"A jerk-off! A thief and a jerk-off!"

"He was a real asshole," Mary chimed in, afraid Sonia hadn't done the man justice.

We climbed the stairs to the second floor, made a slight turn, and stood in the hallway. Before me was Sonia's living room, shielded by long-faded red velvet drapes now yellow with age, and furnished with a sofa, recliner, a few lighted candles for fragrance, a statue of the Blessed Virgin on the corner table, and "I Love Lucy" on the TV. Down the hall at the front were the two rooms Sonia rented to her girls, and the staircase to the third floor. I leaned over the railing and craned my neck to see the room in which Hengleman the rookie had lived. Impossible. He'd need two periscopes and a mirror to see anything.

There are virtues to small towns like Atlantic City. You only had to go to three places to meet everybody in town. At lunch you went to the Stanley, which reserved tables in the back for the doctors, tables along one wall for the businessmen, a long table for the lawyers and judges, and a somewhat shorter table in the bar for the reporters. If you wanted to catch up with somebody and missed him at lunch, you drifted by Angelo's barbershop in mid-afternoon, where everybody got their hair cut, their shoes shined, and their bets down with the bookie at the desk next to the shoeshine stand. If you still didn't find your man, you were bound to trip over him at the President health club, where cops, doctors, businessmen, lawyers, judges, and politicians gathered at the end of the day.

Nobody exercised in health clubs in those days. You went there for the whirlpool, or to be wrapped in a sheet and lie on the chaise lounge in the steam room, or to study the Playboy fold-outs in the sauna while you waited for your rub. Jake ran the men's club with the help of his son and his brother. His wife ran the woman's side with the help of their daughter. Jake being a devout Christian and a lay minister, he did what he could to save souls. Every now and then, with a look of patient hope, he'd open the door to the sauna, say "I thought you might want to hear this," and slip a tape player with a cassette of a sermon or bible-reading on to the bench. You could simultaneously rouse the lust in your heart with *Playboy* and listen to preachers tell you how to find Jesus.

Hengleman the rookie didn't know it, but by the time the trial came up all the reporters, firemen, judges, lawyers, doctors and businessmen had long since tried him *in absentia* over lunch at the Stanley, over haircuts and shoeshines at Angelo's, and through the steam and sermons at the President health club. The verdict was unanimous: He'd stolen the shoebox, and it was about the crummiest thing they'd heard of in a long time.

When the trial began, Hengleman was the guiltiest-looking guy in the courtroom. His fellow cops had already gotten all the publicity they wanted out of Sonia's, and most of them were genuinely ashamed of the new boy. The judge was for Sonia, the jury was for Sonia, the prosecutor was ashamed to be prosecuting the case, and the bailiffs eyed Hengleman like something that crawled out of the sewer.

Things went quickly, although there were a few moments of light-hearted fun, such as when Hengleman admitted it took him two and a half months to gather sufficient evidence to be sure he was living in a whorehouse. With reluctance he also admitted that yes, there were curtains in the hallway and no, he didn't always keep his door open because, well, yes, he dated women, and yes, he'd brought some of them home to his room at Sonia's and closed the door behind him and may have not heard all the parts of the transactions below.

"Pigs!" Sonia snorted. "Pigs! The sluts he brought to his room! I was ashamed to have them in my home!" By then the jury was yawning and deciding whether to vote not guilty and go home to lunch, or have lunch on the State and vote not guilty afterwards.

Hooted out of court, Hengleman the rookie slunk home with his tail between his legs that afternoon, where visitors were waiting for him. After getting First Count to do a little work on the side, I'd had a talk with Jack Jenner, the motorcycle cop. He hated crooked cops more than he hated broccoli. I'm not sure exactly what Jenner said when Hengleman showed up, but from First Count's account it apparently ran along the general lines of: "Listen, fuckhead. The IRS will pay me 10% just to rat on you. Now let's go to your uncle's boat, lift up the back seat, move the life jackets, and get the goddamn shoebox, like it shows in the pictures First Count took yesterday when you were out here counting the money!"

He'd blown some of it, but we got the rest back for Sonia. A gracious gesture on behalf of all the honest cops of Atlantic City. Sonia never did tell me how much was in that shoe box and I didn't peek. Neither did Jack Jenner. As he pointed out, the less you know, the less you have to sweat out grand juries, prosecutors, and ethics committees. For all I could swear, that shoebox was full of Sonia's collection of baseball cards. Of course First Count lived up to his nickname while the three of us drove over to Sonia's to return the shoebox. The low whistle he gave suggested the baseball cards must have included his favorite players. Sonia slipped him a serious slice of it and guaranteed a free room whenever he wanted it. Jack Jenner went back to his motorcycle, Hengleman quit the force, and I went back to my law office assured of a steady supply of beautiful clients who couldn't seem to avoid hanging out with people of bad reputation.

Chapter 8

January settled down after Sonia's case. The TCA informed me the Skin Game couldn't be reached until April. There were "scheduling conflicts" – a polite term for the fact that two of the cops who'd be needed to testify against Frank had been indicted and were busy preparing their own defenses. There was the usual buzz at the Stanley restaurant, at Angelo's and at the President Health Club that we could solve all our problems if we could get casinos. But nobody had the energy. Still, things never stay quiet long. On my way to visit Columbus Wesley, a dishwasher currently in the city clink charged with a Saturday night bar room fight, I stopped by the city courtroom.

City courts are where the action is. The state courts can play with half-day, two day, or two month trials all they want, but city court trials average three minutes. When the day starts, the docket's got one or two hundred cases on it, and the courtroom's packed with bored cops, drunks, nervous traffic offenders, pimps there to bail out their labor force, and lawyers lounging against the wall fly-fishing for clients.

That morning, as usual, the Honorable Bart Morris was on the bench with Solly Rosenblum the bail clerk sitting at his feet like a faithful mutt, culling the previous night's catch. The racket they had going was as sweet as it gets. When a cop busted somebody, the

Honorable Bart was the guy who set the bail – unless it happened at night, in which case Solly set the bail under Bart's authority. If your bail was set at, say, $5,000, you had to put up $5,000 with the bail clerk. Few people have $5,000 handy, so instead you buy an insurance policy. If you skip, the bonding insurance company has to pay the $5,000 unless they can track your ass down and deliver it and the rest of you to jail. The premium's 11% ($550 for those too slow to do the math) which you pay Jake the bail bondsman. Theoretically, Jake kept $50 for his services, and sent the $500 to the insurance company. Once you paid that $550 you never got it back, even if you showed up for court and were found innocent. It was like buying fire insurance and never having a fire.

In Atlantic City they had a different way to skin the suckers. Jake the bondsman kept $150 and kicked back the other $400 to Solly the bail clerk, who divided it $200 to the Honorable Bart and $100 each to himself and to the cop that busted you. It was what the psychobabblers call a win-win-win situation. Everybody won except the insurance company, who never knew bail had been posted under their name, and the defendant, who didn't know he'd been had and couldn't have done squat about it anyway. How sweet it was. And in my innocence I didn't know a damn thing about it.

Fortunately, when I got there Sam-my-Rabbi was on center stage, handling a massage parlor bust in which the undercover cop had just testified. Sam was deep into his cross-examination.

"So you went in, paid twenty-five bucks, and asked for a massage?"

"Yes, sir."

"You got the massage, didn't you?" Snickering from the courtroom.

"Yes, sir. She massaged my genitals, too." The cop wanted the essentials on the record.

"Did she massage your shoulder?" Louder snickers.

"Yes, sir."

"You didn't ask her not to massage your shoulder, did you?"

"No, sir. I figured that was part of the massage."

"Did you ask her not to massage your genitals?"

"No! I mean yes! I mean no! I didn't mean for her to . . ." By now the crowd was richly enjoying things. Sam always put on a good show. The Honorable Bart, deep in consultation with Solly on bail matters, paid no attention.

"Well, what's wrong with her massaging your genitals? You paid for a massage, didn't you? And she gave you a massage. You got what you paid for, right?" By now the courtroom was rocking with laughter at the cop's discomfort. The widest grins came from the first three rows, which is where his fellow cops sat waiting to testify in the next cases. The Honorable Bart, realizing he'd let things go too far and that Sam had gotten enough on the record to win any appeal, found the masseuse not guilty and went on to the more profitable questions of setting bail.

Sam was still in the courtroom when I tried to get my guy released without bail . . . a forlorn hope if ever there was one. The Honorable Bart set the magic number at $5,000 and the dishwasher was on his way back to the cells before I could blink. Sam hustled me into the hallway before I said anything foolish. That's when he explained the facts of life about bail in Atlantic City.

"All you can do is appeal. Takes the rest of the day, but you'll get him out."

"What's the going rate?"

"For an appeal on bail? Don't charge less than $500."

"That's as bad as the bail."

"Yeah, but it goes to pay your rent, not Bart's vacation expenses." Long years had taught Sam the futility of fighting the system. He'd learned to make the best of it, and was trying to pass the lesson on. I headed down to the cells to see my client, dropping the fee for an appeal to $250 as I went. It was going to take me a few years to toughen up.

Columbus was a young black guy with a pregnant wife and a two year old daughter. Watching him through the bars, I saw the tears in his eyes when I told him the situation.

"I ain't got it, man! Ain't got no $550 for bail, an' ain't got no money to pay you for an appeal. An' if I ain't back to work tonight, they gonna fire me!"

I left with the kind of smoldering burn that always gets me in trouble and met David Horsen for lunch. Dave was the judge the politicians had appointed as a stick-on deodorant. Once he was on the bench, the Chief Justice quickly moved him up the ladder. Now he'd been appointed top judge for the two-county area. He had a sense of justice and was looking to make changes. To do that he needed young lawyers to raise the necessary hell that gave him political cover. He was working his side of the street and hoping I'd work mine.

Blowing off steam, I told him what I thought of the Honorable Bart and Solly the bail clerk. He listened intently. Dave's legal experience before going on the bench had been centered on big money corporate cases. The world of city court and bail bondsmen was as foreign to him as central China.

"You've got nothing you can prove," he pointed out. "Without proof, there's nothing I can do."

"I guess not."

"You know, maybe there is," a wicked gleam came into his eyes. "Not directly, but something. There's a program I was reading about, out in Illinois or Indiana, where they set up a system. The defendant still pays 10% of the bail, but he pays it to the court, and he gets it back when he shows up for trial. It cuts out the bail bondsmen completely. And with the court having to account for the money, it cuts out any chance of kickbacks."

"Can we do that here?"

"If you get the information and draw up the procedures, I think I can get the Chief Justice to let me run it here as a pilot program."

After a week of frantic phone calls, intense legal research and frenzied exchanges of drafts, the Chief Justice okayed the program. Without hesitation, Dave called a meeting in his courtroom to announce the new system. Front and center at the meeting were Jake and two other bondsmen. Next to them sat the Honorable Bart, Solly the bail clerk, and three guys from the cop's union looking really pissed. When Dave announced the new program, there was a stunned silence. The lesser hoods looked to the Honorable Bart to take the lead. He turned white as a sheet knowing his cash cow had just been slaughtered, but did his best to save the day.

"But Judge," he sputtered. "This is going to turn criminals loose on the streets!"

"Oh, I don't know, Bart," Dave smiled sweetly. "They're not really criminals, are they? Aren't we supposed to presume they're innocent?"

"But they'll never show up in court!"

"Of course they will! It's worth money to them to show up. That's where they get their bail back! Let's try it for a year. If it doesn't work, we can always change it."

I never saw one man enjoy sticking it to another like Dave enjoyed sticking it to the Honorable Bart and his sidekick that day. Dave may not have spent much time in criminal court, but he knew a gang of crooks when they sat in front of him.

Chapter 9

"I'm tellin' ya, no nigger can join the Antlers! Ya gotta be of the white, caucasian race. It's the law of the Antlers! An' no wimmin neither!" Three hundred pounds of neck fat, massive shoulders and a beer belly bigger than the keg it came from gave the man a natural authority that brooked no argument.

The sign outside the bar said Frank's Pale Dry Café, but the name everybody knew it by was Sambo's; a side-street place on New York Avenue whose back dining room offered the best sandwiches in town, was open twenty-four hours, and was the after-shift choice of every cabbie, dancer, waiter, cop and hooker in Atlantic City. If you wanted a really good Turkey Club at 4 in the morning, Sambo's was where you went.

During the day, the front bar catered to a select crowd of shot-and-a-beer drinkers, guys with dirty necks and dirtier shirts, and the finest collection of racist numbskulls on the east coast. It was a bit on the ripe side but where else could you get the Law of the Antlers right from the horse's mouth? Lunch broke the pattern a bit, with mailmen, clerks from the stores on Atlantic Avenue, visiting salesmen, and the occasional lawyer to add tone.

Sam the rabbi and I were having lunch at Sambo's in hopes of picking up some juicy details about that morning's raid on the Antlers lodge, which was next door over the Armory.

I'd been in city court that morning arguing a weighty case involving whether my innocent had run the red light at Boston and Atlantic. The serious legal issue in the case had nothing to do with the facts. The light had been red, and my client had zipped through it blissfully unaware of the police car lurking on the intersecting street. "Aha!" you will say. "How's he going to get this sucker off?"

The law's changed since then, so I can give away this particular trick of the trade without losing future fees. Traffic lights, like jail space, are governed by mysterious forces invisible to laymen. Deep in the labyrinth of state laws lay an old chestnut that provided in clear and useful terms that nobody could be convicted of running a red light unless that red light had been approved by the state Department of Transportation. On the other hand, the DOT had no power to place a red light on its own initiative. That was the exclusive right of the city governments. The DOT and the Atlantic City Council seldom saw eye to eye on when and whether to install red lights. Keep in mind that fines for running red lights go to the city treasury, not the state. As Deep Throat told Bob Woodward; "Follow the money!" For years greedy cities and townships cluttered the landscape with convenient money traps disguised as stop signs and red lights. Eventually the state realized you couldn't get from here to there without a stop light every sixty feet, and passed the law requiring state approval before traffic lights could be installed.

There came the snag. Swamped by requests for approval of traffic lights by all 536 towns, cities, and hamlets, the DOT processed them in geological time. Ask now, wait a few generations until the state sends a traffic engineer to see if you really need it, and eventually you can hang the red light.

On the other hand, angry mothers of kids on bicycles want the lights right now. Angry mothers vote and the DOT doesn't, so city councilmen learned to skip the technicalities and just install the lights. What driver running a red light questions its right to be there? Would you? You know you ran it; you know the cop saw you do it; and the only reason you'd hire a lawyer would be in the faint hope he could sweet talk the prosecutor into dropping the charge to something less harmful to your car insurance rates.

My rabbi, Sam Goldstein, was a staunch old bull of a lawyer with a permanent Florida suntan who brought his pudgy frame back from Southern golf only long enough to pay for his next vacation. He'd taken a liking to me, I think because he got a kick out of watching me torment the political hacks he'd had to put up with over the years. Sam had a magic list; the locations of the forty or fifty traffic lights in the county that had never been approved by the DOT.

Once he decided to spend more time in Florida and less before the Honorable Bart and his ilk, Sam sent me the occasional case, swore me to secrecy and let me copy the list. Oh, the sweetness of having a heavy-footed driver come in with the ticket that would put him over the top on points and cost him his license, and being able to assure him that for an – ahem – reasonable fee it might, just might, be possible to beat the ticket and save his license. This legal legerdemain consisted of opening my desk drawer and taking a discreet peek at the magic list. Nothing in my tender conscience troubled me about making money the easy way. I'd fire off a letter to the DOT asking confirmation that particular light had never been approved, then show up in court, confirmatory letter in hand, and squelch the prosecutor with an utterly unbeatable defense.

Which was exactly what I'd been doing that morning under Sam's tutelage at the city court in front of the Honorable Bart. The Honorable, still burning for revenge over the new 10% bail program, wanted nothing more than to find my clients guilty, guilty, guilty, every time. He tried keeping a stone face, but I saw him gnash his teeth when I hauled out the DOT's confirmatory letter and used it to tow my defendant out of the treacherous legal swamp of Bart's court.

Before Bart could come up with words withering enough to match his baleful glare, Solly Rosenblum the court clerk stepped up to whisper something in his ear. A rustle in the courtroom spread the news. The State Police had just raided the Antlers' lodge and confiscated its financially lucrative but wholly illegal slot machines.

Unfortunately for the Honorable Bart, he was President of the Antlers, as he'd been for the past decade, during which his take from the illegal slots had almost equaled his cut of the now-defunct bail racket. Even more unfortunately for Bart, the Chief Justice had recently decided to crack down on abuses in the city and township courts by ordering tape recording machines installed. The recorders, by design, had no erase buttons. So when Solly Rosenblum whispered in the Honorable Bart's ear his words, picked up by the nearby mike, achieved instant immortality.

Forgetting the new contraption and assuming they still enjoyed the privacy of the old days, they engaged in a whispered exchange that soon became a classic.

"Jesus Christ, Bart, they're raiding the fuckin' Antlers!"

"They're what? Who?" The Honorable Bart's face could not conceal the horror of his fears. First the death of the bail racket. Now this. What next?

"They confiscated the slot machines!" Solly had grown so calloused dropping bad news on defendants he had no handy phrases to sugarcoat the disaster.

"But those are brand new machines! I just bought them!" Bart protested, oblivious to the fact that he'd just recorded proof of his own guilty purchase of illegal gambling equipment – a serious admission for any citizen and no help at all for a sitting judge.

Recovering from the initial shock, he looked at the clock, saw it was coming up on noon, and banged the gavel to declare a recess for lunch until two o'clock. Sam, whose civic orthodoxy was highly superficial, drew immense pleasure from the Honorable Bart's embarrassment. He raised his eyebrows and suggested we head for lunch to Sambo's so we could get the whole story.

As we walked past the Antlers to enter Sambo's, Bart and his faithful sidekick scurried by, hesitating only briefly before climbing the stairs to the Armory's second floor, where the ceremonial regalia of the Antlers stood, symbol of a defeated and shamed guard, over the small tables on which had once stood the pride of the Antlers, the shiny new slot machines.

The raid was unremittingly bad news for the Honorable Bart and his nearest and dearest. The State Police, still riding high from their Oscar-winning film of the cop selling his motorcycle, had pulled the raid with no notice to the locals; a breach of professional courtesy unheard of in the old days. The word around Sambo's was that the regional superintendent of the State Police was a distant nephew of Sonia's and out for revenge. New Jersey's like that. Our state motto is: "May the knife in your back be your own."

In raiding the Antlers, the state cops struck at the very heart of the crumbling remnants of civic pride. We didn't have much in the way of social elán, but such as we had was in the Antlers. Everybody who was anybody belonged to the Antlers and their wives belonged to the Ladies of the Antlers. The fingerprints on those slot machines represented the social register of the town. More to the point, the state cops had the fingerprints on the little doors and boxes from which the day's take was always personally removed – by the President of the Antlers.

When court resumed at 2 o'clock, the Honorable Bart was back on the bench, the ever loyal Solly at his side. Only then, his eye falling on the mike, did the full dimensions of his problems hit home.

"Erase it!" he ordered Solly. A few minutes of frantic fumbling followed.

"I don't know how," Solly muttered as the courtroom got restive. Hurried consultations and exploration followed, in full view of a courtroom now tuned in to Bart's dilemma and enjoying it immensely. At last the Honorable, with judicial clarity unusual for him, announced his conclusion:

"It doesn't have an erase button!"

"Who the hell would make a tape recorder without an erase button?" Solly demanded.

The Honorable, having learned his lesson far too late, kept his mouth shut and angrily gestured for the next case to begin.

Chapter 10

While these entertainments unfolded in Atlantic City and rumors of legalized casinos grew and spread, Spring crept gradually in from the south. The cherry trees blossomed in Washington, D.C.; fishermen from Cape May to Long Island scraped, caulked and painted boats; and daffodils bloomed at the courthouse in Mays Landing, home to the criminal jury trials. According to the trial list that arrived in the mail, it was time to pick a jury for the Skin Game trial. I contacted Frank Satterlee at his mother's. To my considerable surprise, he hadn't jumped bail.

Mays Landing is a lovely country village at the head of the Great Egg Harbor River, which winds in from the bay and meanders up twenty miles or so before it gets too shallow for anything except inner tubes. The town was founded in 1679 by the first man to navigate the river to its head, one Captain May, or Mey as some insist, who brought his men ashore and promptly incorporated them as the Atlantic County Regular Republican Organization. They have voted in every election since, including a generous sprinkling of Mays and an equal number of Meys. Over the years, the town grew from its humble beginnings to a town of 5,000 inhabitants, 12,000 of whom vote in every election.

The public buildings consisted of the Surrogate's Office, County Clerk's Office, the Courthouse, the diner and the Mill Street Pub. There was also the county jail, which included the office and home of the County Sheriff. In this home the Sheriff's son grew up, eventually to become the State Senator, the first in the history of the county never to be indicted, investigated, or even accused of corruption. Several observers of New Jersey politics believe it would be a good idea to raise all public officials in a home which also houses the county jail, as an aid in the development of their moral character.

Inhabiting the courthouse is a species of hereditary Republican trolls known as bailiffs. These stumpy, craggy-faced creatures, male and female alike shaped along the lines of a barrel with sore feet, earn their daily bread by reading the paper, drinking coffee, and saying "mornin', yerroner" whenever the judges pass them in the corridor. Their countenance is forbidding but they have good hearts, and solemnly inform every young lawyer he is the best they've ever seen.

In the steeple over the Mays Landing Courthouse hangs a bell, which is rung whenever a jury reaches a verdict. Usually, the time between the jury leaving the box and the bell ringing is long enough for all parties to have lunch, after which the bell rings, the jury returns its guilty verdict, and we all start picking the jury for the next case.

That's the theory. In fact, you get a lot of slack time at Mays Landing, partly because country towns don't like too fast a pace, but mostly because nobody knows how long a jury's going to kick things around before coming back with the verdict. If they milk it for a free lunch, the bell won't ring until early afternoon, and by the time everybody's rounded up and the foreman announces the bad news it's past two o'clock, the judge is debating whether to take a drink and then a nap or the other way around, and it's too late to pick a jury for the next case. So orders go out for everybody to report next morning bright and early, unless, of course, next morning is a Friday, which is sentencing and motions day, or one of the 365 holidays commemorating everything from Veteran's Day to St. Barrabas Day.

I drove out to Mays Landing, going from the cold mist drifting in from the ocean and covering Atlantic City, across the tidal meadows to the mainland, the sun brighter and warmer every mile of the way. In early Spring the people inland are sporting tans while the folks on the Boardwalk are still wearing overcoats.

More than the weather changes when you drive inland, even the twenty miles or so to Mays Landing. Atlantic City's a resort town. Sin City, up all night, filled every Summer with Boardwalk hustlers, sunburned lifeguards, college girls waiting tables, and Canadian schoolteachers down for a vacation fling.

Out in the county, once you get past the long, wooded strip of high-priced suburban homes that fringe the bay looking out across the salt meadows from under the trees, you reach farming country. Corn, Jersey tomatoes, watermelons, peaches, blueberries, pumpkins, cucumbers, potatoes, tractors, horses, old trucks, great sprays of water flung about irrigating fields, wildflowers waiting to be plowed under, pine trees, oaks, junipers, maples, all populated by deer, rabbits, dogs, and here and there a solitary farmer working his endless rows, planting, tending, harvesting, minding his own business.

Simple, honest farmers. The sort of practical folk who saw to it the county seat was located in the middle of their farms two centuries back, and have beat the city slickers every time somebody tries moving it to Atlantic City. The business men, insurance companies, and their lawyers once pushed through a proposal to build a new county courthouse in Atlantic City. Out of the fields, pitchforks at the ready, stormed the farmers of Mays Landing. They took that fight all the way to the U.S. Supreme Court, and won hands down. Which is how we ended up with the compromise. Civil trials for money could go ahead and be heard in Atlantic City for the convenience of the lawyers, but criminal trials – and all the clerk's jobs, sheriff's deputy jobs, and jail jobs that go with them, stayed with the simple farmers of Mays Landing.

Of course, there's a downside to having your little town be home to the criminal trials. There are, for one thing, the friends and witnesses of the defendants. Since almost all the defendants are young black men from Atlantic City, the white gentry of Mays Landing find themselves staring at folks given to stronger language and stranger clothing than found on the usual farm. God knows what the black guys from the

Northside of Atlantic City think when they find themselves plunked down in the middle of green lawns, petunias, and white people carrying shotguns and ropes in the back of their pickup trucks.

An even bigger downside for the farmers is the threat of jury duty. The need for picking a jury is one of the dicier things about living in Mays Landing. If they come up short, the Judge orders the Sheriff to send his deputies out onto the street to bring in people to put on the jury. So the farmer heading for the hardware store or the plumber going to fix somebody's sink might end up getting two bucks a day while his work goes undone. Such jurors react badly to long, drawn-out defense tactics. Very badly. Fortunately, the jury pool we had was large enough that we could avoid irate farmers and short-tempered plumbers.

Dearly as we all love the jury system, there's no denying that your fate will be decided by a group of folks none of whom were bright enough to come up with a good excuse to get off that jury. Raffaelli's refusal to believe the coughs, tears, and pleas of lost jobs, hungry babies and doctor's appointments was tough to overcome. My favorite was Juror Number 4, an ordinary guy caught up in the legal seaweed. "Now is there anybody else who has any reason he or she should not serve on this jury?" Raffaelli demanded. Number 4 scratched his head and looked like he was working up courage. Raffaelli glared at him. "Number 4, is there any reason you can't serve?"

"Nossir, but I'm tryin' awful hard to think of one!" He brought down the house.

Chapter II

When driving back and forth from court or office to home, I devote myself to perfecting my life's work: the Donovan Theories. Physicists have tried for years to come up with a Unified Field Theory that explains all the forces of nature, including relativity, gravity, electricity, quantum mechanics and the Democratic Party. What the Unified Field Force Theory is to physicists, the Donovan Theories are to philosophy. I don't say the work's done. Far from it. Students will labor for years to dot the "i's" and cross the "t's". But I'm giving them a hell of a running start.

There is, for example, the Donovan Dimension. This is a measure of such profound social significance I don't know why the Nobel Prize isn't in my bank account by now. The Donovan Dimension is a measurement based on the TFJ – the Time to the First Jackass. Used with proper scientific training, it can give you a quick and reliable idea of the quality of life of any given time or place. Let's take traffic as an example. You leave the house, turn a few corners, and come out on the main road. Start the clock and time how long it takes before you encounter an old geezer hogging the road at 10 miles below the limit, or before some yahoo pulls out of a gas station and zooms up to within two feet of your back bumper, or until a jackass coming the other way drops his cigarette, grabs for it to save his nuts from catching fire, and swerves into your lane. The measurement of Time to the First Jackass is what I call the Donovan Dimension. In summer back then, the Donovan Dimension used to get down to 15 seconds. The day the first casino opened it dropped to a half-second, and it's been getting shorter ever since. But in winter in Atlantic City in those days the Time to the First Jackass was about 2 minutes. For comparison purposes, along the coast in Maine after Labor Day it's still about an hour and a half.

In addition to the Donovan Dimension, there's the Donovan Theory of Eighty/Twenty Nuttiness. This theory is based on the old 80/20 rule. In practicing law, only 20% of the problems clients have are unavoidable. The other 80% are produced by sheer wackiness. Let me give you an example.

The Skin Game trial was set to begin Monday. But now it was Friday night, and our poker game was rolling along nicely. If I needed a ten of clubs to fill an inside straight, I took one card and it was the ten of clubs. If Burnsie had a straight, I had a flush; if he had a flush, I had a straight flush. It was the kind of night when your only regret is that the game limits are quarter and half, and the most we let anybody lose on any night is $100, after which you're on the bench until the next week. Unless you've been on a roll for three weeks and have soaked the hell out of the rest of us, in which case kicking you when you're down is okay. I was $60 ahead and going for the gold. The big loser was Tom Duncan, who never got a pair of Aces that didn't make him chuckle. The man didn't know what the words "poker face" meant. Every time he'd laugh, we'd fold. When he looked grim and tried bluffing we piled on, getting revenge for a winning streak that had carried him damn near a month.

"What's it cost to dissolve a goddamn partnership?" he asked, watching his three of a kind getting murdered by two straights and a full house.

"You and Jim been partners twenty years!" Burnsie pointed out. "Why get your nose out of joint just because you can't play poker worth a shit?" Tom and his partner, Jack Ryan, had started a house cleaning business years before that had grown nicely over the years into a small home renovation and fire restoration business, specializing in the kind of heavy cleanup and quick repair you need when the hurricane takes out your living room or the kitchen range catches fire. It was the smoothest partnership in town. Jack did the bookwork, estimating, and schmoozing with the insurance adjustors to get the business. Tommy ran the crews. They played golf every weekend, and between fires and hurricanes took quick trips to Myrtle Beach where they could get in 36 holes every day for a week.

"Dammit, Tommy, here I am on a roll and you wanna talk business?" I groused.

"Just askin'," he watched me sweep in the pot with frustrated resignation in his eye. "I can't take the son of a bitch anymore." A deep silence fell over the table. Breaking up a partnership like that was the local equivalent of Henry VIII telling the Pope he wanted a divorce. Tom and Jack had grown up together. They'd married sisters; bought houses on the same block. Their own kids had grown up in as tight-knit a family as you could find this side of Louisiana, which doesn't count because when Louisianians marry sisters, it's their own sisters.

"All right. Gimme a call tomorrow." I went back to relieving my friends of their dough while the brotherhood of the poker table divided their attention between saving the partnership and saving their asses.

Next morning before heading for the office I tried getting to the bottom of the partnership problem. Nothing made sense. Both wanted to split up; neither would tell me why. "What is it? Do you think Jack's cheating on the money?" I asked Tom over the phone, ever mindful of First Count's advice. "Nah, he ain't that way." I called Jack. "Do you think Tom's doing work on the side with partnership material?" "Nah," he snorted with deep contempt, "he ain't that way." Stymied, I'd resigned myself to digging through the form books for partnership dissolution papers when the phone rang.

"Donovan, this is Barbara. Kathy and I have to see you before these assholes kill each other." Kathy and Barbara were the sisters Tom and Jack had married. I had them come to the house while I nursed a second cup of coffee.

"So what's going on?" I asked when they showed up.

"It's golf. It's that fuckin' golf!" Kathy said.

"Golf? What's that got to do with breaking up their partnership? Those guys have been playing golf with each other since forever. Now they hate it?"

"No," Barbara said. "Now they just hate each other!"

"It was that goddam hole in one did it!" Kathy said.

I leaned back. There's a moment in every case when the truth heaves into view. This felt like it. "Tell me about it," I said, hardly daring to breathe. Barbara took the lead.

"You know that 12th hole at Brigantine?"

"The par 3?"

"Right. It cuts over the edge of the water, with the two sand traps?" I nodded. Having been in all three on numerous unhappy occasions, I had considerable familiarity with the topography involved.

"Well, they were playing two weeks ago. Now you know Jack's better than Tom. Always has to give him six strokes?"

"Ye-eess," I answered, trying to follow the plot.

"Well," Kathy picked up the narrative, "Tom uses Pinnacles, and Jack uses Top Flites."

"I'm with you so far."

"Tom was having a lousy day. He lost three balls on that water trap on the third, then two more in that creek on the fourth, and another in the lake on the ninth. Then he lost another in the weeds on the eleventh. That was his last one. So when they got to the twelfth, he had to borrow some balls from Jim."

"What, Jack wouldn't lend them to him?" I was incredulous.

"Of course he did! The problem was all Jack had to give him were Top Flites. So they were both playing identical balls. By that time the fog had started comin' in, and when they tee'd off on the twelfth, Tom couldn't see where his ball landed, except they both thought it had to be really close to the hole. Then Jack did the same thing; hit it right towards the cup before it got lost in the fog. They both went up to the green "

"And there was only one ball," Barbara finished, "and the damned thing was in the cup! One of them got a hole in one, and they don't know which one, because they were both using Top Flites."

"Ho Lee Shit!" This was the kind of stuff that could start major wars, let alone bust up a partnership.

"Jack, being an asshole," Barbara went on, speaking of Kathy's husband with Kathy's vigorous assent, "insists that it's got to be his hole in one because he's a better golfer!"

"And Tommy, being another asshole," Kathy and Barbara were unanimous in their assessment of their husband's innate equality, "says Jack's full of shit, and that he's sure that ball's his."

"And now they're gonna fuck up everybody's life just because they're too stubborn to back off! For two cents I'd stick their 7 irons up their asses!" Kathy believed in direct action. "Use the 3 irons! They're longer," Barbara offered.

"All right. Let me think about it," I said. "They didn't cover this shit in law school."

"You won't let them break up the partnership?"

"What, and have to defend you two for murdering your husbands?" They left, reasonably sure I'd find a way. If I didn't, the poker game was shot, my reputation was shot and, judging by their thoughts on the subject, I'd probably end up at the bottom of the water trap with their husbands.

I headed for the office with a sinking feeling that dental school would've been the right choice.

In Hollywood lawyers work all weekend prepping for the big trial. In real life, you spend the weekend doing as much as you can to avoid malpractice claims from neglected clients who don't give a damn about somebody else's trial. You may notice I handled a lot of divorces. Don't assume they made me rich. Take it from me, you can go broke taking divorce cases when you do it on a down payment and pay-me-by-the-week basis. In the short time since I'd hung out my shingle, I'd been swamped with women who made the down payment and skipped the weekly follow-up. That's when I learned that the courts didn't care if you got paid. Once you took a case, you were in it to the end, whether you got paid or not.

So I went in on Saturday to catch up on the divorces. Harry Castleman held the elevator door for me with his usual courtesy, and a twinkle of approval for a young lawyer working weekends. Harry wasn't the oldest lawyer in town, but he was close. The only two older than Harry were "Ducky" Richardson, admitted in 1907, and "General" Drobors, '09. But Ducky only kept his number in the phone book. He hadn't been seen on the street since he gave up his office. "General" Drobors kept an office in the Guarantee Trust Building, but he only pottered in once or twice a month to water his plants. The Guarantee Trust was home to a dozen old duffers like the General, not as old but seriously up there, living comfortably by gently milking the estates of long-dead friends. Every now and then you'd round a corner in a corridor and see one of them staring out the window, trying to remember whether he was coming or going.

Harry Castleman was made of sterner stuff. He came in at 8 o'clock every weekday morning, nattily dressed, spotless tie perfectly in place, and worked until 5, throwing in a few more hours on Saturdays. He'd been admitted in 1911 – when Woodrow Wilson was still Governor of New Jersey debating whether to take a run at the White House. It was a fading but still common practice for lawyers to travel from Atlantic City to Mays Landing by horse and buggy, putting up for a week or two in the hotel to try cases during the session, as Harry had. He was a class guy from his highly polished shoes to his perfectly trimmed gray hair, and I liked him. He'd worked steadily and invested his earnings in real estate. The real estate was in Pennsylvania and not Atlantic City because he liked keeping his investments private. The word was that he owned about half of Pittsburgh.

"Tim, could I talk with you a moment?" Harry asked me with the grave courtesy that was his hallmark. I followed him into his office, which was next to mine. Mine had been his friend Ducky Richardson's office until he gave it up, which may have encouraged Harry to offer me the use of his library whenever I needed it. When I did, he always took a few minutes to see how I was making out, and I always took advantage of his time to ask how things had been in the old days. It's fascinating to talk with the real old-timers. Pieces of living history. Like the Atlantic Leatherback turtle I'd seen one day while fishing way out in the ocean with Manny Gottinger. Manny, who knew all there was to know about construction (since he'd built about half of Atlantic City), and fishing (since he'd been fishing for 70 years) cut the power so we could drift to within a dozen yards of the ancient turtle. "Going from its size and looks, I'd say that turtle's about 120, 130 years old," Manny said. I was looking at a creature that had been swimming when Lincoln was still practicing law in Illinois. Harry Castleman was the Atlantic Leatherback of the Atlantic City Bar, still swimming a hundred years later. Manny Gottinger had two brothers. One was a doctor. The other was Harry Castleman's law partner.

"Tim, I'm thinking of closing the office," Harry Castleman said, leading me into the library and closing the door behind us. "I thought you might be interested in buying the books." He gestured to the lawbooks, shelf after shelf, neatly stacked in glass-fronted bookcases.

"I can't believe you're closing up shop. Is everything all right?"

"Oh, yes. I've always been blessed with good health."

"Getting tired of it after all these years?"

He smiled. "No. Actually, between you and me, I plan to keep working out of my apartment. Lillian," he nodded to the outer office where his secretary of 50 years was typing away non-stop, "will come work with me there. But I have to close the office. Can't see any way to avoid it."

"Why?"

He hesitated, then faced the hard part. "It's Gottinger. He's in a bad way, and I don't have the heart to just break up our partnership. It'll be easier if I tell him I'm retiring."

He didn't have to say any more. Harry Gottinger was the junior partner in the two man firm, having been admitted in 1917. Like Castleman, Gottinger came to work every day, perfectly dressed, staying from 9 to 5. But he'd long since drifted into a world of his own. His work day consisted of sitting in his office, lost in some long-gone time, until the sounds of closing roused him to put on his hat and coat and head out the door.

"I just can't do it to him," Harry Castleman shook his head. "I doubt if he even remembers who I am half the time. But how can I tell him after all these years that I want to end the partnership? If he realizes I intend to keep practicing, it would be the end of him."

"Harry, I'd love to have the books, but I'm just getting started. I can't make you a decent offer."

He shrugged that aside. "I don't need the money. I'd just like to see you get some use out of them. How does a hundred sound?" Harry's collar may have been starched but his heart wasn't. We were talking about books it would've cost upwards of $5,000 to buy. My protests did no good. "I'll let you know when we're moving," he said. "It won't be for a couple of months. Send me a check when you get around to it."

I looked around at shelf after shelf of books, in perfect condition, neatly arranged in the old glass-fronted oaken barrister bookcases antique dealers drool over. "I'll have to get some boxes," I said, thinking along the lines of the grocery store's thick cardboard jobs.

"Oh, take the bookcases," Harry insisted. "I've no use for them once the books are gone."

"Harry," I was almost speechless. "those shelves are worth more than the books. I can't take them!"

"Well," he looked at them. "I bought them sixty years ago from old George Butler when he was retiring. I think I paid him – well, I forget. Tell you what. We'll say $100 for the books, and another $100 for the shelves. How's that sound?"

"It sounds like I'm taking you to the cleaners."

He looked at me with an amused glint in his eye. "If you are, you're the first man that ever did," he answered wryly, changing the subject. "How's your practice going?"

I told him about the Hole-in-One problem. Having been partners with the same man for sixty years, he saw the serious side of the damned thing. "I don't play golf myself," he said. "But during the Depression I invested in a bankrupt country club and it turned out well. The manager's been working for me for years. Perhaps he'll have a suggestion."

He called, and with the same dry precision he'd use in discussing a commercial lease, described the problem, got the answer, thanked the man, and hung up. "Not much help, I'm afraid," he turned to me. "Apparently under the Rules of Golf you are not permitted to borrow equipment from another player. When the one fellow ran out of balls, he was disqualified from further play. Nothing he did thereafter can be counted."

"So Jack gets the hole in one?"

"I'm afraid not. A second Rule provides that a Hole in One is not recognized unless you are playing as part of a foursome. I believe these fellows were playing as a twosome?" I nodded.

"So Jack technically gets the Hole in One but not officially?"

"Well, no," Harry sighed. "There's a third Rule that applies to the situation. If you can't positively identify your own ball, then it's considered lost and you must take a penalty stroke and tee off again."

"So both guys would be considered to have lost their ball?"

"Evidently. It would seem that, applying the Rules strictly, neither of them can claim that Hole in One."

We sat in silence for a moment, two lawyers reluctant to see a perfectly good partnership break up. "Of course," he said, eyeing me shrewdly, "there's always the Law of the Case."

The Law of the Case! I could've hugged him, starched collar and all. He'd rummaged around in his mental attic and dusted off a legal rule so old it had whiskers when Shakespeare was looking for an empty stage. I'll skip the Latin footnotes. Among its more obscure virtues is that, whatever the law is outside the courtroom, if the parties to a lawsuit agree on a particular interpretation of a relevant point of law to govern their dispute, that interpretation becomes "The Law of the Case." Can't be used in any other case, isn't worth a damn as a precedent, but it's binding on the parties to that case and the judge can use that interpretation to decide that case.

"If they stipulate as the Law of the Case that a ball that appears to be the one they struck off the tee is presumed to be their ball, then instead of being lost – " Harry speculated,

"They both get a Hole in One!" I was on it like a hawk on a field mouse.

"Naturally, you'll have to get them to agree," Harry pointed out.

"I did tell you these guys married girls who are sisters." He nodded sagely. Nobody ever had to spell things out for Harry Castleman.

Armed with the Law of the Case, it didn't take long to settle matters. I didn't even have to talk to Tom or Jack. I told their wives, who cheerfully and promptly knocked sense into the numbskulls. Kathy made her husband buy Jack a plaque commemorating Jack's hole-in-one. Barbara made her husband Jack buy the same thing for Tom. It was that, or divorce court. They bitched about it, but I noticed each kept his plaque hanging on the wall of their mutual office.

Chapter 12

After sweating out the Hole in One problem, the Skin Game trial offered a certain relief. Whatever offenses Frank might be guilty of, playing golf wasn't one of them.

Squeaks planned to produce all 22 victims as eyewitnesses to the stickup, and as many cops as he could round up as eyewitnesses to the shoot-out. At least three of the questions he'd be asking each and every one of them were: "Did you see who did it? Is he in the courtroom?" and the final "Would you point him out, please?" I knew damned well that over the next few weeks 25 or 30 fingers would end up pointing straight at Frank Satterlee. My only hope was to argue that any identification they made of him now wouldn't be based on their independent memory of the event, but on the prejudicial effect of seeing my innocent lamb dragged before them in handcuffs as if he were guilty; a prejudice strengthened by the fact that the Press had printed the photographs of Frank in handcuffs with such prominence that it was now impossible for any of the witnesses to make a separate, reliable identification of Frank as the real gunman. There was, of course, the purely technical difficulty that Frank *was* the real gunman. But why quibble over technicalities?

Squeaks had his own problems; mostly concerning the quality of his witnesses, all but 2 of whom had done serious time for everything from aggravated assault to attempted murder. This was good, solid stuff I could use to slash, cut and burn their credibility once I got to cross examine them. The two with no records were more troublesome. Squeaks led with them.

The jury, fresh and curious about the case, always listens to that first witness with depressing attention. In this case it was Big Dingy, or Washington Cullen as he was called on the witness list. He was a fat, solemn man, never seen without a necktie or with a smile. He'd never been arrested, convicted, charged, or suspected of any crime. Big Dingy was the houseman; the dealer who ran the game and kept the players honest, in return for the house cut of each pot. In church, he was known as Deacon Dingy – the only man fully trusted to count the collection money. He looked the part. Wearing a starched white shirt, dark tie, and a conservative black suit, he waddled slowly to the witness stand, stood patiently, rested his hand on the Bible held out to him by the clerk, took the oath, and made himself comfortable in the witness chair. Any hope that he might be the type to skitter around a bit with his testimony disappeared the minute I got a good look at him. He was about as nervous as a man riding the bus home from work. He told the story of the stickup with the steady voice of a man ordering pepperoni on his pizza, and stolidly pointed a fat finger at Frank as the lead gunman.

It seemed prudent to get Big Dingy off the stand as soon as possible, in hopes that by the time we reached the last witness the jury would forget whatever the first one had said. When a witness is clear, believable, and nailing your guy to the wall, the dumbest thing you can do is try to trip him up on cross-examination. All that does is burn his testimony into the jury's memory. On the other hand, you've got to do something to raise some skepticism on the part of the jury. I've seen old pros in that situation glare at the witness with great suspicion and demand in a skeptical voice whether he'd ever lived anywhere else, then dismiss whatever answer came with a contemptuous "No more questions!" as if the witness had something to hide.

Before I let Big Dingy go, I had to come up with a throwaway question, just to let the jury know I was in there fighting. If he'd been dealing for three or four hours, as seemed likely, the jury might buy a closing argument that he'd been so tired by the time of the stickup either his eyesight or his memory wasn't up to snuff. On the other hand, if it turned out he'd only been dealing for a half-hour, I'd argue he hadn't been dealing long enough to be sure my guy wasn't one of the cardplayers instead of one of the gunmen. It seemed safe enough either way it went, so I asked:

"Mr. Cullen, how long were you dealing that game?"

"Twenny-seven years."

"Twenty seven *years?*" I blurted out, stunned. The laughter from the jury box confirmed that he'd handed me in three words all that I needed to alert them to the fact that this game was under police protection, that if the cops didn't catch the stickup guys nobody was going to pay for that protection any longer, and that maybe my guy was nothing but a scapegoat grabbed by the cops and paraded before the outraged victims as the alleged robber. All this in three unexpected, delightful words from the placid, unshakeable Washington Cullen, a/k/a Big Dingy.

"Twenny-seven years," Big Dingy repeated.

"You mean to tell this jury that illegal card game has been going on just a block away from the Police Headquarters for twenty-seven years?" I wasn't about to let this gem go unpolished. Raffaelli, with the wisdom of years of experience, knew that the Prosecution's case had just hit a major pothole. He coughed and glared pointedly at Squeaks.

"Your Honor!" Squeaks was on his feet. "I object! There's no relevance! It doesn't matter how long that game was going on!"

"Of course it matters!" I wanted this stuff banged into every juror's head. "The jury has every right to infer that game was under police protection and the police were desperate for a scapegoat when they arrested my client!"

Raffaelli was livid. "Mr. Donovan! There's not a shred of evidence to support any inference of police corruption!" The gavel got another workout, I got another baleful look, and the jury got its orders: "The jury will draw no such inference as defense counsel has suggested! It makes no difference whether that game had been going on for twenty-seven minutes or twenty-seven years!"

The hell it didn't. The looks on the faces in the jury box said it all. And in his eagerness to get the knife between my ribs, Raffaelli had managed to accomplish two things I dearly appreciated: He'd forgotten to strike Big Dingy's basic statement about the 27 years from the record; and he'd made such a big deal about those 27 years, the jurors would be telling their great grandchildren about it fifty years later.

I could have challenged Big Dingy's identification of Frank as the testimony of a man who'd been running an illegal card game. But folks take illegal gambling about as seriously as jaywalking and cheating on your taxes. It was that 27 years I needed. I got Big Dingy off the stand without further ado.

Aside from Big Dingy, Robert Gifford, better know to his fellow cardplayers as "Shipyard," was the only victim of the stickup who wasn't burdened with a serious criminal record I could use to attack his testimony. Shipyard, a tall, vigorous old oak with gnarled hands, weathered features, and that deep, gravelly kind of booming voice old-time sea captains used in hurricanes, was a born raconteur. Squeaks stepped him through the stickup or, to be more precise, asked him what happened. Shipyard took it from there. With that unforgettable voice, rangy body, down-home accent and perfect timing, he filled the witness chair like an actor in a one-man play. And with a captive audience, a judge leaning over attentively to hear him stick it to my client, and the spotlight all to himself, he was having a ball. He told about the card game. He told about the hands he'd lost, and he told about the seat he sat in. He shrugged away Squeak's occasional questions as impertinent. Not that they were needed anyway. This was his story, and he wasn't about to let himself be interrupted. The jury lapped it up.

"Mr. Gifford," Squeaks finally got in when his man paused for breath. "Did there come a time when the defendant addressed you?"

"Yeah! They come a time when he say to me . . ."

"Which defendant was this, Mr. Gifford?"

"That one there! The big one! The one at the end of the table!"

"Your Honor, may the record reflect that Mr. Gifford is pointing to the defendant Frank Satterlee?"

"Yeah, that's him! Frank Satterlee's the one that said it. Man stuck that shotgun right in my face! 'Bout two inches from my eyeballs!" He paused for dramatic effect, which gave Squeaks a chance to get in another question.

"And what was it the defendant Frank Satterlee said to you, Mr. Gifford?"

"Told me, he says: 'Get your mothafuckin' hands up against the wall!' "

Squeaks flinched and cast a worried look at the several lady jurors to see if any of them showed signs of fainting at the bad language. Turning a bright pink, he tried to move on.

"I s-s-see. And what ha-ha-happened next?"

Shipyard, until now producer, director and starring witness in this courtroom drama, was dumbfounded. "Whutcha mean what happened next?" he demanded angrily. "Man had a shotgun at my head! I got my mothafuckin' hands up against the wall! Thass what happened next!" He stuck his hands up as if the gun was right in front of him.

"Order! There will be order in this court!" Raffaelli pounded his gavel furiously, trying to stop the howls of laughter. "There is nothing in this case that should provoke the jury to laughter! I will not have it! Order in this Court!" The jurors, several of whom had their handkerchiefs out wiping tears from their eyes, ignored him. Raffaelli banged away with his gavel, getting madder and redder by the minute. By now thoroughly unnerved by the situation, Squeaks reverted to form, turned scarlet and started giggling. Raffaelli, outraged at Squeaks for letting down the side, hammered away with his gavel. "Mr. Prosecutor, I should think you of all people would refrain from this unseemly laughter!"

"Y-Y-Yes, Your ho-honor. Nuh-nuh-no m-m-more que-questions," Squeaks giggled.

The situation was bad, but not hopeless. Here, after all, was an old man who had seen the defendant over a year ago for only a few minutes, and under the most distressing circumstances. There was nothing to stop me from trying to create in the jury's mind the sort of reasonable doubt about the accuracy of his memory that comes in handy at the end of the case when you make your closing arguments. Of course, some crafty groundwork would be needed. It would be suicide to pick a fight with him. He already had the jury eating out of his hand. Best to try the warm, friendly, "I understand how confusion can affect the memory" approach.

"Mr. Gifford," I started out, "do you have any nicknames?"

"Sho I do! Everybody got a nickname. That's how you tell folks from cops and bill collectors." This was an easy man to like.

"What are you called?"

"They calls me Shipyard Slim. That's 'cause I worked in the Shipyard. Sometimes they calls me Chester Slim, on account of I lives in Chester. Mostly they calls me Shipyard."

"Do you mind if I call you Shipyard?" I cozied up to the old ham.

"No, I doan mind."

"Shipyard," I asked, full of fake sympathy for this ancient relic. "How old are you?".

"Seventy-eight, somethin' like that."

"And you are retired?"

"No suh!" he boomed. "Ain't never gonna retire!" From the vigor of his answer, it looked like he was good for another twenty years. So much for the ancient relic.

"Where do you work?"

"You mean my day job or my night job?"

"Order! Order in this court! The next person on the jury who laughs will be held in contempt! Mr. Shipyard! I mean Mr. Slim! No, I mean Mr. Gifford! Do you mean to say that you work two jobs?"

"Yessir Judge. Daytimes I work at the Holiday Inn."

"You may proceed, counselor."

"And what hours do you work there?"

"7 a.m. to 4 p.m. – six days a week."

"That's a long day. What sort of work do you do?"

"Cook."

"You have a night job on top of that?"

"Yup. Cook at the Holiday Inn in Philly. 6 to 9."

"Shipyard, are you telling us that at the age of 78 you work from

7 in the morning till 4 in the afternoon in Chester, then drive to Philly and cook for another 3 hours?"

"I didn't say nothin' about drivin' to Philly! I doan drive. My woman drives me."

"Okay, your wife drives you from one job to the other."

"Didn't say nothin' 'bout no wife! I said my woman drives me!"

Raffaelli shot a warning glance at the jury, most of whom were trying hard not to laugh out loud.

"And on the day in question – the day they stuck up the Skin Game – did you work both jobs that day?"

"Yessir."

"And you went from Philadelphia to Atlantic City after your second job?"

"Yessir. Went to Skin. Skin every night somewhere."

"How far is it from Philadelphia to Atlantic City?"

"Bout an hour, bit more. That's when I sleeps."

"Did your woman drive you?"

"Not that woman. My other woman!"

Raffaelli didn't even try to gavel down the laughter at that one. "Would counsel approach the bench?" Baldheaded, thick glasses, bucktoothed and scrawny neck, he did his best to look judicial as he leaned over the bench to whisper his questions.

"Mr. Donovan, where are you going with this line of questioning?"

"Well, your Honor, I'm going to show that the witness was so exhausted by the time the robbery happened that he mistook my client, who came there to play cards himself, for the robbers who shot up the place."

"Very well. I will allow it. He certainly has a strenuous schedule. My oh my. Two women. 78 years old. You may proceed. I think we'll recess for lunch at the next logical break."

"Now then Shipyard. Where were we? – Oh Yeah – you were saying that you have a second woman drives you to Atlantic City to play cards?"

"Yup. Do that three, fo' times a week."

"And she waits to drive you back home?"

"No not her. My other woman."

"You mean the woman who drives you from Chester to Philadelphia comes down to drive you home from Atlantic City?"

"No, not her. I got me an Atlantic City woman. She drives me home."

The gavel exploded. "I will remind the jury of what I previously said about laughter! This is a courtroom, not a theater!" Raffaelli peered over his glasses at Shipyard with growing envy.

"Now Shipyard, do you follow this schedule every night?"

"Yes, Counselor. Exactly! Mr. Gifford, I must say I have seldom heard of such a schedule at your age. Do you take any vitamins?"

"No sir, Judge. Doan take no medicine, doan drink, an' doan smoke. Ain't never been sick a day in my life."

"Thank you" Raffaelli said weakly. "Mr. Donovan?"

"Yes, your Honor. Shipyard, do you really play Skin every night? Isn't it expensive?"

"Only if you loses. I always Skin."

"And you always win?"

"Ain't nobody wins forever. But I sit down to Skin, I got a thousand dollar stake, see me through okay. Take a thousand everywhere. Never know when yo gonna find a good game. Got a thousand on me right now!" He put his wallet on the witness rail with a proud flourish.

"All right ladies and gentlemen. We will recess for lunch until 1:30. Counsel and defendants will remain seated until the jury leaves the courtroom." When they left, Raffaelli called us to another sidebar.

"Mr. Donovan, I was watching your client's face when Mr. Gifford pulled that wallet out, and I didn't like what I saw! I'm quite certain he intends to get his hands on that thousand dollars. I don't think Mr. Gifford's safe with him on the street. I'm revoking your client's bail."

"Judge – you can't – you can't do that!" We finally worked out a deal. A court bailiff volunteered to have lunch with Frank and keep an eye on him to make sure he did not get to Shipyard. Frank was to remain at the courthouse under guard an hour at the end of the day to give Shipyard a head start getting home. Frank, after a long, expressionless stare, agreed. Squeaks and I headed across the street for lunch at the diner.

I started the afternoon session still determined to undermine Shipyard's identification of Frank Satterlee. Shipyard returned to the witness stand with the gusto of a great actor called back for an encore before an enthusiastic audience.

"Shipyard," I resumed the questioning, "when all this happened, did you have your money on the table?"

"Sho' did."

"How much money?"

"Dunno exactly. Four, five hunnerd."

"And did the other players have money on the table?"

"Course they did."

"So there could have been several thousand dollars in cash on that table?"

"More'n likely."

"Now Shipyard, you know the dealer, Mr. Cullen pretty well?"

"Big Dingy? Sho'. Knowed him 'most thirty years. Best houseman anywhere."

"And it was Big Dingy's job to look out for cheats?"

"He ain't the only one. I doan care who's dealin'. I always keep my eyes open."

"Now as we talk today, all this happened months ago, right?"

"Yep."

"And at that time, months ago, the whole thing lasted – what? 20 or 30 seconds? You're 78, get very little sleep, worked two shifts that day, rode over a hundred miles, played cards for several hours in a crowded room, and after all that, with your money on the table, three men came in with guns, and shouted at everybody to get their hands up against the wall. Somebody got hit with the butt of the shotgun, the light got shot out, the table with five or six thousand dollars in cash got knocked over, and there were 25 or more men in that room, everybody trying to get their money and get out. Isn't that the way it happened?"

"Yeah. Was a helluva night!" He seemed downright nostalgic.

"Okay, Shipyard. Now here's my problem. Suppose my client came down just to join the game, and got caught in that stickup. How can you be so sure that this is the man who did the stick up?

"How can I be sho?" He played the jury like a comedy club audience, with me as his straight man. "I tell you how I'm sure! That man stuck that shotgun right in my face, I looked up the hole of that gun and it was the biggest hole I ever seen in my life! And I says to myself, 'Shipyard, that's the last man you ever gonna see in this world, so look on top of that hole and get a good look at him!' And I did! An' I ain't never gonna forget him! An' thass him, sittin' right thar!" The jury was convulsed with helpless laughter as he dramatically pointed a long, bony finger of a big, rough hand at the end of a long, ropy arm right at Frank Satterlee. The old bastard was loving every minute of it. So was Vinnie Raffaelli, who let the jury have their laugh before gaveling things back to order. He watched me trying to pull the harpoon out of my chest with a gleam of malicious satisfaction.

"Any further questions, Mr. Donovan?" Raffaelli poured salt into the wound.

"No thank you, your Honor. In view of the witness's age, I see no reason to burden him any further." It wasn't much, but sometimes you have to shoot back, even when all you've got for ammunition is a marshmallow. "In defeat, defiance!" as Churchill said. I got sympathetic grins from two of the jurors.

Chapter 13

I drove back across the farmland and the tidal marsh as battered and bruised by Shipyard's testimony as if Frank had been innocent. But the further I got from Mays Landing, the more I mellowed. After all, Shipyard hadn't done anything but tell the truth, although I wished the jury had heard the truth from the mouth of a mumbling nitwit rather than from the booming voice of that likeable old rogue.

It didn't take long to convince myself that, with a stop at the appropriate watering hole and the help of a Drambuie or two on the rocks, I could regain the old confidence and be ready to face the morrow. This excellent plan was foiled only by my foolish decision to stop at the office first. In these modern times it wouldn't matter, because bad news can get to you by cell phone anywhere. But in those days you had to meet bad news halfway, which is why so many lawyers had their drinks before going back to the office after a day in court. I didn't and I paid the price.

Did you know there's actually a club for optimists? It's true. They have rules, and meetings, and pay dues – a bunch of smiling idiots who go through life insisting there's a silver lining behind every cloud. Try finding the silver lining behind the clouds when the hurricane comes ashore on your street. My secretary was waiting for me with the usual pile of letters to sign, bills to pay, phone calls to return and a look that told me she was waiting for the right moment to break the bad news.

"What?" I asked.

"Anna Ruby."

"Oh, shit!" Such is the mental shorthand that grows between lawyer and secretary.

Anna Ruby was a tough old bird who'd enjoyed a long and active career as a supervisory nurse at the City Hospital. She'd seen it all; quadriplegics in the war, drunks extricated from car wrecks, gunshot wounds, emergency-room births, drug addicts and schizo's. She'd trained generations of nurses to deal with the unbalanced wheel of tragedy and farce we call an urban hospital.

Long since retired and eventually bed-ridden in a nursing home, she'd decided to make out her will. Her nephew, a friend of mine, suggested my name. So months earlier I'd gone out to Our Lady's Residence and gotten the particulars, routine except for the trust fund she wanted set up for "Code Blue," her pet cat.

Making provisions for a pet to be cared for is no odd thing. People do it all the time. Unfortunately, as a lawyer drafting my first will, I hadn't the faintest idea of what practical problems to anticipate. You can do a trust for children, knowing the money's going for their education, doctors, or whatever until they grow up. But a cat? I mean, how old was Code Blue, and how long was it expected to live? Was it female? What if it had kittens? Should they be included in the trust, like grandchildren? Laugh if you will, but the list of things they didn't cover in law school was getting longer every day.

I was certain there must be hundreds of handy cat-trusts in the form books. Having resolved to visit the law library and come up with the finest cat-trust ever drafted, I placed Anna's file conveniently on the right side of my desk, to be sure it wouldn't get lost. There it slowly sank from view under the later arrivals of divorces, bankruptcies and drunk drivers.

And now Anna had been taken from the nursing home to her old hospital, where she lay dying, her will undrafted, unsigned, and sitting unformed somewhere at the bottom of the pile.

After a day with Shipyard, the last thing I wanted was to spend the early evening frantically drafting a cat-trust. What I wanted was a honey-colored, sweet, cold, comforting Drambuie on the rocks, with just a twist of lemon rubbed lovingly around the rim of the glass. But duty is duty, and malpractice claims disturb one's sleep. So I did the cat-trust, and I did the will, and to make sure I had an extra witness for the will signing I called First Count, who had left Legal Services and was now working for me full time. We rode the hospital elevator up debating the odds as to whether the old lady was still alive.

The hell of small town law is that there are no secrets. We got off on the fifth floor and immediately ran into Arlene Lisynski – whose mother Maggie had helped my mother out with the ironing. Her brother Tommy was a boyhood playmate of mine who'd ended up working as an elevator mechanic. In an alcoholic haze he'd stepped twelve floors down into an open shaft and eternity. Arlene had gone to nursing school and spent her early professional years under the tough but loving tutelage of Anna Ruby.

"How is she?" I asked. There was no mistaking the look of cold reproof in Arlene's eyes.

"On the tubes and oxygen, if that's what you mean," she said.

"But still alive?" My heart was in my throat.

"Barely." It didn't matter how long we'd known each other. Arlene was giving no comfort to the incompetent nitwit who'd screwed up in the matter of Anna's will. "She's in 509."

I walked down the corridor with the heavy step of a man headed for the gallows. In Room 509 a grim collection of white-uniformed veteran nurses stood watch over Anna – a supine figure lost in the austere sheets, tubes, bottles, and other horrid mechanics of modern medicine. I moved to the bed, convinced my entire legal career was doomed, and feeling guilty enough to warrant the hostile eyes that watched me lean over Anna. She didn't seem to be breathing.

"Anna," I said, "can you hear me?" An eternity passed.

"Ye-es-sss," came a low, laborious rasp. Thank God! She was alive! She was conscious! My ass was saved! Now to establish that she was lucid enough to sign her will. I leaned over the tubes and IV bottles.

"Anna, do you know who I am?" First Count and the covey of nurses leaned forward to hear the answer.

"Yo-ur-rr my law– yer." She forced it out.

"And do you know why I'm here?"

"Yo-uv'e got my wi-ill." Her lips barely moved, but I could hear every word.

"I certainly do!" I answered, master now of an awkward situation. I turned, pumped up with relief and newfound salvation, motioning to First Count to hand me the will. Suddenly the rasp started again, slowly picking up volume behind my back.

"And-yo-ou-to-ook-your-God-damned-time-a-bout-it!"

Anna hadn't lost the old vim. First Count pursed his lips, trying to keep a straight face as he handed me the will. The squad of nurses didn't even try.

"Boy, she's a tough one!" First Count chuckled, going down in the elevator. "I thought that ol' lady was dead, but seems to me she's probably gonna last a while 'for she goes."

He was right. She lived another five years in the nursing home, and told that story to every nurse who ever came to visit her.

The cat? Lived to a ripe old age in Florida with Anna's grand-niece, last I heard.

Chapter 14

"We gotta talk," Frank greeted me next morning, steering me to the nearest bench in the courthouse square. "Some stuff's goin' down. Calvin skipped, an' there's somethin' goin' on with Eddie's lawyer." The bailiff waved us inside before Frank could continue.

Calvin Williams and Eddie Jones were our two co-defendants. Both had been seated with their lawyers and Frank and I among the crowd at the defense table the day before when Raffaelli announced his impulsive decision to revoke Frank's bail. Although I had managed to stave off that disaster, Calvin, who was also out on bail, had listened keenly to the controversy. Realizing how uncertainly the winds of freedom blew in Raffaelli's court, when court adjourned for the day Calvin shot a knowing look at Frank and departed for parts unknown.

This was bad news. Aside from the fact that it might tempt Raffaelli to revoke Frank's bail again, Calvin's lawyer was the man the Public Defender was talking about when he promised "my guy will help you out" in my first jury trial. I watched with glum foreboding as he picked up his briefcase with a happy smile, wished me luck, and left.

Raffaelli declared a short recess and busied himself with the fun of issuing a bench warrant for Calvin's arrest. My remaining colleague, Eddie Jones's lawyer Herman Schalick, known throughout the Bar as

"Hemorrhoid Herman" busied himself with arranging the little air-inflated rubber tube on which he sat to relieve his hemorrhoids. Frank, contemptuously watching Hemorrhoid fuss with the device, leaned close to me.

"C'mon outside. We gotta talk," he said. Where Frank led, I had learned to follow.

Once outside, Frank looked around the flower-bordered green lawn with a hint that distant pastures were beginning to look good to him. I was afraid to ask if he was thinking of skipping.

"What you think of Eddie's lawyer?" Frank asked.

"Not much," I admitted. I didn't know him well, but Hemorrhoid's years of experience had not won him much respect among the brethren. Guys who'd tried cases with him told me he wasn't the kind of guy to irritate judges by jumping to his feet with objections, or even questions. He figured he was getting paid by the State so they could pretend his client had a lawyer. All he had to do was show up, keep his mouth shut, and collect his pay. Except for the occasional outbreak of hemorrhoids, it was a cinch.

"Eddie ain't sure what to do 'bout him."

""He can't be that bad," I commented. "He's been around for years. Must've learned something. Why? He wants to get somebody else?" Eddie was the only defendant who had neither escaped nor raised bail, and was resident in the county jail. His only hope of getting back on the street someday lay with his appointed counsel. Unfortunately for Eddie, you don't get to be too choosey about which Public Defender you get. He'd drawn Hemorrhoid Herman, and he was stuck with him – and his little rubber ring.

"He told Eddie's wife she's got to put out for him if she expects him to work up a sweat 'bout Eddie. If she don't give up some pussy, Eddie's gonna get 5 or 10 years more'n he should."

"Son of a bitch!" I was still new enough to be outraged. "Is she here? I'll take her in to see the judge. She doesn't have to put up with that crap! Neither does Eddie." I rose to go inside.

"Sit down, my man." Frank caught my coat. "Don't do nothin' dumb. She ain't about to lay down for that old turkey. He probably

can't get it up anyway. But there's somethin' Eddie wants to know."
From his tone, I sensed the kind of stunt Schalick was trying was more
common than I could have dreamed. The day would come, I promised
myself, when I was going back to law school and teach a course on
how things really work.

"What's he want to know?"

"S'ppose he don't say nothin'? What if his old lady never told him
'til after the trial? That be enough to get him a new trial?"

"Hell, yes," I said. "But why wait? He can get a mistrial declared
right now. He'd get a new lawyer, and the whole thing would start
over."

Frank displayed tolerance for the rookie. "Thing is," he pointed out
patiently, "I told him he don't want to start over now. Gettin' a new trial
a year or two from now be more to his likin'. Ain't no tellin' how many
of them witnesses gonna still be around then. That old Shipyard gotta
die someday, the way he keep goin'. Big Dingy, he so fat ain't nothin'
but huffs and puffs, could drop dead tomorrow. I told Eddie could be
he waits a couple years, gets through on an appeal, cuts hisself a deal
on a new trial, and gets out early. How's it make a difference whether
he say somethin' now, or he wait and see?"

I didn't like it, but I had to agree Frank's thinking was sound.
Maybe he should teach the course. He certainly had a strong grip on
the realpolitik of the law.

"Frank," I said, "Remember this is my first jury trial. I was counting
on Calvin's lawyer to give me advice as we go along. With him gone,
and Schalick being worthless, you may want to ask the Public Defender
to assign a more experienced guy to take it from here."

He looked at me with what I took to be appreciation for my candor. "Naw, you doin' fine, my man." I was touched by his confidence. It
means a lot to a young lawyer.

Chapter 15

W hen the buzz over Calvin's disappearance settled down, we got back to work. Frank and Calvin had been the gunmen in the action. I'd been counting more than I realized on Calvin's lawyer to carry the weight for the defense. With Calvin on the run and his lawyer cut loose, I was left with Schalick as senior man at the defense table. But I couldn't bring myself to sit next to that sleazy son of a bitch and his hemorrhoids. At the counsel table, I kept my client and his co-defendant Eddie Jones between myself and Schalick. In any event, he didn't plan to do much except sit on his inner tube and hope for the best. His client had stayed in the alley as lookout and never actually entered the stickup room. None of the holdup victims would be able to identify Eddie Jones, and only two of the cops would identify him as running down the alley. Except for the embarrassment of being caught with three of the victim's wallets on him, Eddie still had hopes of getting off and, his ace in the hole, a later appeal based on the Schalick gonads.

Shipyard was a tough act to follow. Once he was gone, Squeaks followed no particular order in putting his platoon of aggrieved victims on the stand. Between their direct testimony and my cross examination, we were ploughing through the witnesses at the dizzying pace of two a day. Raffaelli chafed and chomped, but I was working on the theory that the more distance I could put between Shipyard's testimony and their verdict, the better chance we had.

Spring burst forth in full glory as the succession of witnesses trooped to the stand, recited their catechism, and pointed their fingers at Frank. After Squeaks stepped each witness through his story, ending up with their identifying Frank, I'd go through my own routine, pinning down their age, their occupation ("lookin' for work" was the overwhelming favorite), how much they'd had to drink that night, and what drugs they were on. The drug question drew Raffaelli's fire, but I insisted with a straight face that I meant "medicine" and was entitled to ask if the witness's perception had been influenced by any drugs. He didn't like it, but knew he had to back off, especially when he saw the knowing grins on the juror's faces. Thereafter, I'd pause in every cross examination, glance meaningfully at Raffaelli, turn my back to him and with a wry glance at the jury ask the witness: "Were you taking any, ah, *medicinal* drugs that night?" It was the sort of question that made the witness, the Prosecutor, and the Judge all nervous at the same time. I think the jury started to look forward to it with each new witness.

What really got to Raffaelli and Squeaks was when I asked each witness how long they'd been playing the game when the stickup began. No matter what answer I got, I followed up by asking if they'd played in the game on other nights and, if so, for how many years. Stung by Big Dingy's statement that he'd been dealing for twenty seven years, Squeaks and Raffaelli were between a rock and a hard place. If they made a fuss, the jury got it seared into their brains that this was a protected game. If they didn't make a fuss, I got the same result. Almost every witness admitted he'd been a player for years, except when "out of town", which meant in jail.

Basically, I was sticking to the tried and true stratagem of every good defense lawyer: Try to discredit, confuse, and intimidate wherever possible. With some it worked, especially with those who'd done enough time in state prison to realize they might meet Frank back at the ranch someday, where a knife from the guy you pointed your finger at is part of the Welcome Wagon.

Just when the witness thought he was through the worst, I'd reach for my file, thick with the police records of the witness list. "Mr. Brown, have you ever been convicted of a crime?" after which, allowing for the inevitable shyness about such matters, the witness would admit that he'd been convicted of this or that rape, attempted murder, armed robbery or other offense. And, in some cases, that he was at that very moment awaiting trial on such charges and, well, yes, there had been discussions with the Prosecutor about the beneficial aspect that testifying against Frank might have on the disposition of those other matters. By the time we finished going through the police records of Squeaks's witnesses, the jury was looking at Frank in a softer light. Nobody who robbed all these tough nuts could be all bad.

Squeaks, still tender from Shipyard's booming use of the word "motherfucker" in front of the lady jurors, phrased his question carefully when asking what, if anything, Frank had said to them. It did him some good but not much. Especially when he came to Elijah Morton.

Elijah was the hardest of the hard cases. He was the only one of the witnesses who'd done more prison time than Frank, and it was clear from the looks of sheer hatred they aimed at each other that both looked forward to a deep and meaningful conversation when they met again, whether behind bars or in one.

"Yeah, he said somethin' to me. Made us take off our clothes and stuck us in that bathroom. I tried gettin' his shotgun, but I tripped goin' for him and he hit me with it. That's when it went off an' blew out the light. Time I got back up, most everybody was in that bathroom. I hadda take off my stuff and he shoved me in. Said "Git in there and wiggle yo' ass so them other faggots got somethin' to aim at! That's what he said."

Squeaks was in extreme discomfort. None of the lady jurors had fainted, but clearly it was only a matter of time. "N-N- No mm–more questions, Your Ho-Honor!" He headed for the safety of the Prosecutor's table.

I rose to cross examine, being careful not to step in the line of sight between Frank and Elijah. I don't believe in death rays, but why take chances? Each of them was putting out enough energy to blast through the shields of a Federation starship.

There was no hope of weakening Elijah's identification of Frank. Things had been way too personal for confusion or mistake. On the other hand, if I was reading the jury's reaction right, there had grown in their minds a certain sympathetic understanding of the case. Who gave a damn if armed robbers like Elijah were themselves robbed? Maybe this was a score they should be left to settle privately, instead of wasting good tax money sending Frank to prison. There are good reasons why judges and prosecutors deeply distrust juries. Jurors since the time of William Penn in Merrie Olde England have balked at finding people guilty just because the judges want them to. Hell, my own ancestors came over with Quakers who'd been sent right from the jury box to jail for refusing to return guilty verdicts in 1677. Why do you think O.J. walked?

I picked my place carefully, standing at the end of the jury box furthest from Elijah, so he'd have to look toward the jury when he answered, letting them see the desire for violent revenge in his eyes.

"And did you?" I asked, tongue in cheek.

"Did I do what? Wiggle my ass?" The death ray spun around to me, and to the jury. "Hell, no! I ain't no goddam faggot!" Elijah answered before Squeaks could interrupt. I let the answer hang for a minute while Squeaks tried to figure out how to word his objection without getting back to the nasty part about the ass wriggling. Frank was enjoying himself hugely.

"The question was meant as 'Did you go into the bathroom?'," I covered, squelching Squeak's's objection before he could get it out. Several jurors flashed me glances of humorous recognition of what I'd been up to. Long live the Quakers.

"Yeah, I went in. Meet him someday without that shotgun, be a different story, though." Judging by Frank's expression, he was unimpressed with the threat.

"In fact, you had further words with the defendant that night, didn't you?" I asked.

"Nothin' important."

"Isn't it true that when the police were putting Frank into the police car, with his hands cuffed behind his back, you tried to get at him?"

Elijah's court experience was clearly at conflict with his desire to assert his manhood. That bathroom scene had left deep scars. The scars won out. "Yeah, I went after him."

Squeaks was on his feet. "Your Honor, what went on after the defendant was captured has no relevance . . ."

"It has every relevance, your Honor. My client's position is that he came down to play poker and was swept up in the stickup. Any identification of him by these witnesses is prejudiced, based on his being dragged in front of them handcuffed. He was put on display like a man on the way to the gallows! I have every right to cross examine into events that took place between this obviously enraged victim and my client!"

Raffaelli, unsure where I was going but unwilling to risk a successful appeal, denied the objection with obvious reluctance. I repeated the question.

"Yeah. I went after him," Elijah repeated defiantly.

"In fact, you reached into the front seat of the squad car, grabbed a cop's gun from his holster, and tried to take a shot at my client, didn't you?" The jury, after several weeks of boring stuff, was on the edge of their seats.

"Woulda got him, too, if . . ."

Squeaks for once was on the ball. Elijah's admission of attempted murder of a prisoner in custody was not in the play book. "Your Honor, this witness should be advised of his right not to incriminate himself . . ."

"By all means," I snapped. "Let's read him his rights before he admits . . . again . . . that he tried to steal a police officer's gun and murder a handcuffed man!"

Frank snorted with amusement. Raffaelli looked like he'd bitten into an apple and found half a worm. With his teeth clenched and his jaws on triple lock, he gave Elijah the full Miranda. Elijah, who'd heard his rights more than most of us hear the Pledge of Allegiance, paid no attention.

"And isn't it true that after the squad car incident, you went over to City Hall and spoke to the defendant again?" I was on a roll and wasn't about to let up. The man's hatred was steaming out of him like a volcano waiting to blow.

"Yeah, I went there."

"And you spit on him while he was handcuffed to a chair, right? And you had words with the defendant?"

"He asked did I want to suck his . . ."

"Ob–objection! Your Ho-Honor, this has n-nothing to do with . . ." Squeaks was obsessed with the effect of all this on the ladies. Murder, holdups, knifings, all were within social bounds. But such language! No lady should have to listen to it.

"It has everything to do with it," I insisted. "This man is obviously so burned up with hatred of my client he'll do or say anything to put him in prison!"

After another few hours of that sort of thing I let Elijah off the stand. Not, of course, without first hauling out his truly impressive police record and going through it conviction by conviction. Even Raffaelli looked thoughtful at all that. I noticed he did not, as he had with Shipyard, insist on keeping Frank in court for an extra hour to give Elijah a head start for home at the end of the day.

Chapter 16

However mixed their feelings were about Frank sticking up the likes of Elijah Morton, when Squeaks called the first of the police officers the jury tightened up. They knew there were charges floating around about assault with intent to kill police officers, and weeks of testimony about assorted thugs being robbed wasn't going to distract them from the serious stuff. I was not looking forward to Jack Jenner telling them about the scumbag who'd fired five rounds at him. Raffaelli, on the other hand, looked like a kid who'd dutifully eaten his broccoli and was waiting for Mom to bring the ice cream. Rather than have each cop listen to the testimony of the guy who went before him and get ready for my cross examination, I had the witnesses sequestered in a separate room until called for, as I'd done with all the previous witnesses.

Knowing Jack Jenner was his best witness, Squeaks decided to save him for last. Fortunately for me, he started off slow, and slow was the word for George Hanrahan, easily the dumbest man ever to wear a badge. He kept his shoes shined, his uniform clean, and his mind empty. His testimony was classic cop language, the only language he knew. It ran along these lines:

> Squeaks (after establishing name and rank): "Did there come
>   a time when you received a call of an armed robbery in
>   progress?"

Hanrahan: "Yes, Sir." (Glancing at his notes). "I was in Car
43 when a 91 came in. Officer Timmons was with me.
We proceeded immediately to the 23, confirmed the
91, and reported 56."

Squeaks, (looking dazed): "And these are codes?"

Hanrahan: "Yes, Sir."

And so it went. Squeaks worked on him with pick and shovel for a
half-hour, finally digging out that Hanrahan and his partner had answered
the dispatcher's call, gone to the Skin Game, got out of the car, and
were walking up the alley when two other squad cars and a motorcycle
arrived. He saw one man run away from him just as two other men
came out the side door, turned away from them, and ran into the
warren of cramped back yards and high wooden fences that lay behind
the building. While this was going on their attention was momentarily
distracted by the squealing wheels of the getaway car pulling away
from the storefront. Shots had been fired. Hanrahan had drawn his
police revolver and seventy-threed several times.

"You mean you discharged your firearm?"

"Yes, sir. After they fired at us."

"And are any of the men who shot you and ran away from you
present in this courtroom?" Squeaks asked.

"Yes, Sir."

"Would you point him or them out?"

Hanrahan nodded his head in the general direction of the defense
table, indicating that Frank, Eddie, myself and Hemorrhoid Herman
had been at the stickup. At this point the prosecutor usually recites
something like "Let the record reflect the witness has indicated Frank
Satterlee and Eddie Jones." But Squeaks forgot, and I saw no reason to
help him. He may have been afraid Hanrahan would put the finger on
a 7-11. Raffaelli, who could have nailed it down, was busy signing
bench warrants the clerk had lined up for him and missed the moment.

Since Hanrahan hadn't been specific on the identification, I was
free to concentrate on other matters. "Now, Officer," I asked, "this all
took place at, what? One or two o'clock in the morning?"

"Yes, sir. That's correct."

"And you were on patrol in the squad car when the call came from the dispatcher?"

"The 91?"

"Yes, the 91 when you were in 43." I couldn't resist it. Neither could the jury. I could feel the tension go away. How the hell can you take testimony like that seriously?

"Yes, sir."

"What, exactly, did the dispatcher say on that call?"

"He said 'They're stickin' up the Skin Game."

"That was it? That was the entire call?"

"Yes, Sir."

"And you proceeded directly to the Skin Game?"

"Yes, Sir."

"Did the dispatcher state the address of the Skin Game?" Having the imagination of a tree stump, Hanrahan had no clue how important his answer would be.

"No, Sir."

"But you went directly to the Skin Game?" The jury had come to point like a Labrador retriever spotting a duck.

"Yes, Sir."

"And the dispatcher never gave you the address of that Skin Game?" The courtroom was quiet. Hanrahan's answer carried clearly.

"I have no carnal knowledge that he did, sir."

The jury was still laughing when Raffaelli, his face purple with anger, gaveled them into silence. I used the time to get Hanrahan off the stand and out of the courtroom. He's been known around town as "Carnal Knowledge Hanrahan" ever since.

Barry Timmons was next up; a sleepy-voiced, slow-talking man whose main interest in life was the pile-driving business he ran on weekends and vacations. Police work was alright and built up your pension, but Barry was no man to get excited about it.

He was also no man to go chasing armed robbers up a dark alley. The best Squeaks could get out of him was that he'd been in the car, followed Hanrahan up the alley, heard some shots, and saw Frank and Eddie and a third man running toward the back yards.

Cross was fairly straightforward.

"Did you see this man, Frank Satterlee, shoot a gun at you?"

"No, Sir. I was behind my partner. There were a whole lot of gunshots. I got in the doorway and shot four or five rounds back there, but couldn't see what I was shooting at so I stopped."

The jury by this time had pretty clearly grasped that, whatever was going on, and however many shots had been fired all around, nobody had been hit. A few jurors were biting their tongues, hoping I'd ask Timmons why the hell he was shooting at something he couldn't see, but I figured it was damned decent of him to stop, considering he was shooting in the direction of five or six houses where innocent people lived. I didn't press the point. Why kick a sleepy dog?

When we recessed for the day, I found Ted Johnson had parked next to me and was getting into his car. Ted was the reporter who broke the story about the Great Undertaker's War, and was covering the Skin Game trial. On the theory that buying drinks for reporters was a deductible advertising expense, I talked him into joining me at the Mill Street Pub. There are reasonable grounds to suppose he was heading there anyway, reporters, unlike lawyers, being notorious lushes. Three of the jurors saw me, smiled and waved. But aside from a smile and a friendly nod, I stayed away from them. Contacting jurors during a trial would be highly unethical. Also, the odds that half the bar patrons worked for the Prosecutor's office were strong, and there was no sense tempting fate. Still, jurors that go out for a drink after a day listening to witnesses and Vinnie Raffaelli can't be all bad. I took it as a good sign.

"The thing I can't figure," I told Ted when we had our drinks, "is how come nobody got hit. There must have been 50 or 60 shots fired, and that nest of backyards and alleys can't be much bigger than a two car garage."

He took a long pull on his Budweiser, and gave me a cynical grin. "I was there that night, you know," he said.

"No shit!"

"No shit and no subpoena either. Deal?"

Subpoenaing reporters ranks right up there with slamming the car door on your fingers for stupidity. I nodded agreement. "What the hell was it all about?"

"I was riding around in the squad car with Hanrahan and Timmons when that call came," he said. "When we got there, it was the biggest clusterfuck I ever saw. Guys were runnin' around in all directions. Three of those witnesses were running down the street buck naked, yelling for somebody to get them a gun. Four or five had their pants on, and they had guns. They were after your guy before we got there. By the time Hanrahan and Timmons headed down the alley, your guys and the card players were shooting it out. Looked like the fuckin' O.K. corral!" He laughed, taking another swig.

"So it's bullshit about my guys trying to shoot the cops?"

"Not entirely. I know your guy got some rounds off at Jack Jenner, but I can't believe he was trying to hit him. Hell, he wasn't more'n ten feet away. I could be wrong. Those back yards are closed in by high wooden fences, there's no light except the kitchen windows in the houses, and you can bet they got turned off in a hurry!"

"So the cops went in after them?"

"Not on your life! C'mon! Joe LoPresti's two months from his pension, Timmy Stimson's too fat to get his gun out in under an hour – hell, it was his gun Elijah tried to get so he could shoot your guy. He just couldn't reach far enough to get around Stimson's gut. And Jack Baker ain't gonna pull his gun until there's a photographer ready to take his picture. The only guy went in was Jenner, and he was having second thoughts. Why get yourself killed in the dark when you can wait until daylight?"

Much that had been murky now became clear. Johnson was chuckling at the memories.

"You really should've seen it. When LoPresti and Baker came up the alley, LoPresti looks at Baker and says 'Go after them, I'll cover you!' Baker takes one look back there and says 'Fuck you! You go get 'em, and I'll cover!'

" 'Great,' says LoPresti, 'I kill one of them sons of bitches, and I get sued for my ass!' Meanwhile, all the card players by now have their pants on, and they're standing at the alley openings . . . there's at least four different alleys lead back there . . . just shooting for the hell of it. By the time the cops went back there, they didn't know who was shooting. For all they knew, the cops were shooting at each other!"

I looked at Ted. An honest guy, but the fact was none of this stuff had appeared in his stories. One wonders why. Especially when one is me. "What's the deal you made?" I demanded.

Johnson grinned. "It's a protected game," he shrugged. "The cops have been takin' money from it for years. In exchange for not making them look like assholes in the paper, I get pictures of Dick Henley and Bootsie Humphrey in bed together."

Dick Henley was the rising political star, a pillar of rectitude, especially along the white suburban communities. Bootsie Humphrey was a black bombshell, lately taking to putting on a gospel music show on Sunday morning radio. The pictures would never have been published in those pre-Monica days, but God knows what Johnson was going to get in trade when he took those pictures to Henley. Probably a copy of the Governor's little black book and a shot at the Pulitzer. I raised my glass in salute and gratitude.

All this considerably relieved the strain of cross-examinations the next day. Nothing like a map to give you confidence about where you're going. When LoPresti, Timmy Stimson and Jack Baker got on the stand next day, I was able to use my cross to paint a highly accurate, and believable, picture of what had actually taken place. Squeaks watched his cherished charges of assault with intent to kill police officers turn from grave charges to dubious allegations to outright farce.

But he still had the Ace in the hole. He called his best and last witness, Jack Jenner. I watched with deep misgivings as Jack came out of the sequestered room and took the stand. By an odd chance, I caught a flash of recognition between Jack and the Number 5 juror, Kathy Distal – a flash that took me back to freshman year in high school. Jack and I had hung out together for that year, with a couple of other guys and two or three girls. One was Kathy . . . . then Kathy something or other, now married. But the fact was Jack and I both had one of those intense high school crushes on her; the kind that send you off the deep end during the two weeks it lasted. I never was sure whether she liked both of us or either of us or neither of us, but the two weeks passed. At the end of the year, she moved to another town and another high school, and Jack and I moved on to other sweethearts, other lives. Now here we were together again.

In a perfect world, I'd have immediately informed Raffaelli that I knew one of the jurors, and off we'd go to a mistrial and start all over again. I am not, however, perfect. After five weeks of trial, I'd had all of Squeaks, Raffaelli, and Hemorrhoid's inner tube I could stand. So I kept my mouth shut. Shoot me.

Jack, always observant, caught the look of recognition on my face and gave me a sly grin. What the hell. What judges and prosecutors don't know won't hurt them. He'd testify however he was going to testify, I'd do my job, and Kathy'd do hers.

I don't think Kathy had as much to do with it as Hengleman and Sonia of shoebox fame. Jack had been genuinely ashamed of Hengleman; filled with the contempt an honest cop feels for a slimeball who gets on the force. In any event, Squeaks soon found his star witness had a memory with more holes than a slice of Swiss cheese.

"And are any of the men who took shots at you here today in this courtroom?" Squeaks asked.

"I think so. I think he was one of them," Jack pointed at Frank. "Think" is not a word prosecutors welcome in police testimony. "Yes," "Sure", "Absolutely", "No doubt about it" are good, solid old English reliables. "Think", on the other hand, is filled with Hamlet-style indecision; the sort of language in which, as Shakespeare pointed out, "the native hue of resolution is sicklied o'er with the pale cast of thought."

Whatever made Jack hand me this gift, I accepted it gratefully and made the most of it.

"Officer," I began, "You say you 'think' my client took those shots at you. But you're not sure?"

"I was when I filled out my report. But the more I thought about it, it being dark and shots going off all over, I have to say I can't be certain. Somebody was shooting at me, but it coulda been the guy that skipped."

Raffaelli was an unhappy camper. He'd been around long enough to know something serious had slipped in Squeaks's case. Without further ado, he jumped in.

"Officer, do you mean to tell me a man took five shots at you and you can't identify him?"

"Like I said, Judge, I think that's the guy. I just can't be sure. It was dark, and there were shots comin' from all over."

"I fail to understand how an officer can be uncertain who is shooting at him. Especially when he himself is the officer who arrested this defendant."

"Yessir. But that was two hours later. For all I know, the guy could have been shootin' at the card players who were shootin' at him. Or it could have been the other guy. I think it's this guy, but I can't swear to it for sure."

"But you are sure this is the man you found with the pistol, the shotgun, and the loot hiding in a trash barrel two hours later?" Raffaelli was livid.

"Absolutely." Jack was at his best.

"No further questions. I thank the officer for his candor," I said, with an absolutely straight face for which I'm still saying penitential Hail Mary's.

Raffaelli glared, Squeaks looked totally lost, and Kathy Distal had a Mona Lisa smile on her face as Jack stepped down from the stand.

Chapter 17

The closing statement was one of my best. I took my time, hammering at my main themes that the cops, paid for years to protect the game, grabbed the first convenient suspect and paraded him, handcuffed, in front of press, public and outraged victims, then plastered his face all over the newspapers as the man caught with the goods on him, and overall so vividly impressed my client's identification on the minds of the victims that, however innocent . . . or semi-innocent . . . he was, the testimony of all the witnesses was so tainted that the jury was entitled to find a reasonable doubt and thus acquit my client.

Alas, not all of this could be stated quite so directly. It's considered bad form . . . and grounds for disbarment . . . for a lawyer to make allegations of police corruption in open court with no proof to back him up. That's why those familiar with trials chuckle when witnesses swear to tell "the truth" (of which they seldom learn); "the whole truth" (which any judge will prohibit as irrelevant); and "nothing but the truth" (a degree of self-restraint mere mortals seldom display, especially when they've got an entire courtroom listening to them.)

The direct approach was out. But just because a straight line is the shortest way from A to B doesn't mean you can't go the long way. For the best part of two hours I reviewed each witness's testimony in painstaking detail, painting it as clearly the result of crooked cops hell-bent on finding somebody, anybody, to feed to the growling mob. Throughout, Raffaelli watched me like a hawk hovering over a cornfield, waiting for the first wrong move that would let him nail me.

Fortunately, Squeaks helped enormously by jumping up every six minutes to protest that I was impugning the honor of the police force. Since I was doing my damndest to accomplish precisely that but couldn't say so, his objections were an unexpected gift.

"For example, ladies and gentlemen, when you recall the testimony of Mr. Jones, it was that he heard the shots, ran through the plate glass window, ran directly to City Hall, and blurted out to the dispatcher 'They're stickin' up the Skin Game!' You heard the dispatcher testify that he immediately got on the radio to all cars and broadcast 'They're stickin' up the Skin Game!' And you heard each and every officer testify that, upon hearing that dispatch, they immediately went directly to the Skin Game – an illegal card game that, as Big Dingy testified, had been going on for twenty seven years! Yet at no time did that dispatcher give out the *address* of that game. In fact, he never even asked Jones for an address. And from that, ladies and gentlemen, you can fairly infer that – "

"Ob-ob-objection! Objec-jection, your Honor!" Squeaks was on his feet. "Counsel is trying to get the jury to believe the cops were p-p-paid off to protect the game!"

"I said no such thing, your Honor. I would never try to imply, just because the game's been going on for 27 years and every cop who answered the call knew its exact location without being told, that the cops were being paid to protect it. What I said was – "

"We'll hear exactly what you said, Mr. Donovan. I think the Prosecutor's point is well taken, even if he was slow about it. The reporter will read back Mr. Donovan's comments."

It was read back, thus hitting the jury for a third time with the obvious.

"Very close to the line, Mr. Donovan. Very close. This Court will not tolerate such inferences – "

"Of course not, your Honor. I'm sure the jury is as aware as I am that this Court will not let the police be criticized – "

"Mr. Donovan, I'm warning you – "

"I was about to say unfairly, your Honor."

Raffaelli, seeing half the jury trying to hide their grins, subsided. Sensing a good time to quit, I turned to the jury (which effectively kept Raffaelli or Squeaks from seeing my face), lifted my eyebrows and physically wiped the grin off my own face, closing with:

"Ladies and gentlemen. I'm sure, taking everything you've heard into consideration, it will be just as easy for you to find reasonable doubt in this case as it was for the police officers to find the Skin Game itself."

"Ob-ob-obb-objection! Ob-ob-jection!" Squeaks, though nervous, this time got to his feet in time to avoid Raffaelli's fire.

Before Raffaelli could get the froth out of his mouth, I turned and walked to my seat at counsel table with a meek "Thank you, your Honor. I'm done with my statement."

Raffaelli, purple faced and eyes bulging, was deciding whether to risk ordering my remarks stricken. If he did, as he and I both knew, he would thus imprint them permanently on the jury's minds. On the other hand, if he didn't, the chance to nail me would be gone. In the silence, while the jury and I exchanged amused glances and Raffaelli was working his way through the logic of his dilemma, Frank, unaware that his confident whisper could be heard by Judge and jury alike, leaned over to congratulate me.

"Helluva speech, my man! If I wasn't there, I wudda thought I was innocent myself!"

At this, three of the jurors laughed outright. Squeaks sensed he should do something and rose to object, but caught Raffaelli's glaring eye and promptly sat down. Raffaelli, at least, knew a good thing when it landed in his lap. He gave me a look of malicious triumph and turned to what is known as "charging the jury."

This hoary old routine consists of the judge reading to the jury a long list of boilerplate legalese intended to explain to them the difference between guilty and not guilty, inferences, assumptions, presumptions, rebuttals, preponderance, reasonable doubt, unreasonable doubt, and the finer points of six or seven other areas of law. By the time he let the jury go, he'd been reading to them without looking up for an hour and ten minutes, during which time they'd gone from alert to indifferent to bored to semi-conscious.

When at last the ordeal was over and the jury released to their deliberations and the nearest rest rooms, Squeaks and I emerged into the bright sunshine of a summer day and headed across the street to the diner to wait it out.

Squeaks was distinctly uncomfortable at lunch. No sooner had we ordered the soup and sandwich special than he checked his watch. The jury had been out half an hour, the bell had not rung, and Squeaks was convinced from these two facts that he'd end up with a hung jury and be forced to spend the rest of his legal career handling juvenile delinquents.

"C'mon, Squeaks. Relax. All they're doing is getting one more free lunch on the county before they wrap it up."

"I don't know. I think they were really disturbed at the profanity. Do you remember Mr. Gifford's testimony?"

Remember, hell. When Squeaks asked him what happened after Frank told him to "get your motherfuckin' hands up against the wall," Shipyard's "Whutcha mean what happened next? Man had a shotgun in his hand. I got my motherfuckin' hands up against the wall!" the jury had doubled over with laughter. Who could forget that gem?

"Shipyard? Yeah, I have a dim recollection. What bothers you about it?"

"Well, when he used the MF word, I think several ladies on the jury were very offended. I should never have asked the question that way. And that testimony from Elijah Morton about what was said when all those men were stripped and stuffed into the bathroom. I really think I should have done something."

The diner, as is the way with diners, had tried to look good by serving the salad on a plate half the size it required. Cutting it with knife and fork, then retrieving the bits and pieces of lettuce, tomato, onion, and cucumbers that fell over the edge of the plate gave me a few seconds to ponder on how to comfort the poor bastard.

"Squeaks, in the first place there isn't a woman left in the country who doesn't hear worse than that while she's shopping at K-Mart. And in the second place, what the hell could you have done?"

"I could at least have asked the Judge to strike the language from the record. It's been almost 45 minutes since the jury began deliberations. I really should have asked Judge Raffaelli to strike that sort of language. When Mr. Gifford testified and used the MF word I was looking right at Juror Number 5, and she looked absolutely horrified."

"Number 5? Kathleen Distal?"

"Yes, Mrs. Distal. I just know she took strong offence at that. And the jury sheet says she's the mother of two children."

"Jesus H. Christ, Squeaks. Here you've got 27 eye witnesses including 6 cops, each and every one of which personally identified my guy as the main man. They caught him with a pistol and the loot in one hand and a shotgun in the other; and when I finished my closing statement he blew five weeks of work and two hours of my best speech ever by telling me he did it, in a whisper you could hear all over the courtroom; and you think the goddamn jury's gonna let him walk? Squeaks, if they do, I'll be the one demanding a new trial!"

We dawdled over the ice cream, debating whether to order another coffee, when the bell rang. Squeaks twitched, hearing the sound of doomsday. We'd already paid the bill, so I was spared having to pick up the tab. But I held his elbow as we crossed the street back to the courthouse.

Chapter 18

I n Hollywood, Frank would have walked out of that courtroom to a standing ovation from the Jury, while Raffaelli wept and gnashed his teeth. This, however, was Mays Landing.

We stood for the verdict. Frank was by far the most composed. Squeaks was keenly trying to read the expression on Kathleen Distal's face, his nervousness making him vibrate like a tuning fork in high pitch. I wanted to give him a twang just to see if the windows cracked from the high note.

The long reading of the verdicts began, the foreman being asked by Raffaelli as to each count against each defendant. Calvin Williams, absent these many weeks, was found guilty on each count, one after the other. Eddie Jones was found guilty on each count, a verdict to which Herman Schalick paid less attention than he did to adjusting the little rubber ring-seat he used to protect his hemorrhoids.

When the foreman started to read the verdicts on Frank Satterlee, Raffaelli sat up with that gleam in his eye judges get when they fondle the book they're about to heave at the defendant.

Mays Landing may not be Hollywood, but this was obviously a jury that liked Mel Brooks movies. To the first count, of assault with intent to kill a police officer, the foreman loudly announced "Not Guilty". Raffaelli turned to absolute stone. Even I held my breath. To the next 5 counts of assault with intent to kill a police officer, the foreman announced "Not Guilty", then proceeded to announce "Not Guilty" to the first count of armed robbery, and "Not Guilty" to the next, and the next, for what seemed a long, long time. Raffaelli developed a new color for each "Not Guilty" he heard; first pale, then red, then purple, and so on through the rainbow. By the time the foreman had said "Not Guilty" to the 11th count of armed robbery, Raffaelli was a basket case.

But, having had their fun (Kathy Distal giving me a merry wink), the foreman saved Raffaelli's nearly finished life by getting down to business and pronouncing Frank guilty of the remaining 11 counts of armed robbery. They also found him guilty of possession of a pistol, but not guilty of possession of a shotgun. Even Frank broke out in a laugh at that one.

"They pattin' you on the back for a good try, my man. And they sticking it up that ol' judge's ass," he whispered, again unaware of the broadcast quality of his voice. I could but agree silently with his analysis.

"Sorry Frank. Wish we could have done better."

"Doan worry about it, my man. You done your best." Once again, I was touched by his faith and confidence in me.

Chapter 19

Even as Frank worked on his appeal, a threat more serious to Big Dingy and the Skin Game than mere shotguns and pistols was slipping into town. The Little Bo Peep Paint Company of Rahway, New Jersey, newly acquired by businessmen considered (only, you understand, by the ill-informed) to be of the Mafia persuasion, wanted casinos, for which a number of obstacles stood in their way, including the State Constitution, which prohibited them. A statewide referendum to change that had failed a year earlier – largely because it would have allowed casinos anywhere, thereby alarming church groups, environmentalists, and good-government types all over the State. Now that Little Bo Peep had arrived on the scene, they were ready to try again, this time limiting casinos strictly to Atlantic City, which was notoriously short of church groups, environmentalists, and good government groups. In a clear indication they meant to win, Little Bo Peep hired "Triple Dip" Danny O'Brien as their lawyer.

Danny had originally built his law practice by walking up to defendants in the Honorable Bart's court and urging them to hire him, clinching the deal with the straightforward claim that "I'm expensive, but I'm damned good. You get off, or you get your money back!" Such arrangements were forbidden under the rules of ethics of the time, but Danny regarded his fees as nobody's business but his own. His motto was "I don't know much law, but I sure as hell know how to make money at it!"

From these humble beginnings Danny graduated to personal injury work. The math was tricky but the cash moved like lightning. If an old lady fell down her apartment steps – worth $100,000 in those days – Danny's card would be pinned to her dress by the time the ambulance unloaded her at the emergency room. A quick medical report, copy to Mike "Sticky Fingers" Locklin the insurance adjustor, and the claim would settle for $50,000. Of that, Danny took his expenses off the top, carved out a $25,000 legal fee, slipped half of that to Sticky Fingers, and showed up at his client's bedside before the plaster dried on her casts, proudly waving her check for $15,000 or $17,000. True, she could have gotten $75,000 had the case moved according to the Rules of Ethics, but even half-blind old ladies can spot the difference between a real $15,000 now and a highly theoretical $75,000 three or four years from now.

Danny spent large chunks of his rapidly growing capital on politics, the investment of choice for prudent-minded lawyers everywhere. Soon he was appointed receiver for a bankrupt nursing home, whose legal bills promptly jumped from $5,000 a year to $150,000, plus expenses. From there it was only a hop, skip and jump to get himself appointed district auditor for the Estate Tax, a political plum that required him to take inventory when the grieving heirs gathered hopefully to open the safe deposit box at the bank. By the happiest of ethical loopholes, nothing prevented Danny from suggesting, in cases where the box contained sufficient loot, that the heirs needed an estate lawyer like himself.

His marketing talents drew public frowns and private envy from the organized Bar until a naive Committee Chairman from North Jersey assumed that any man handling that much Estate business must be good at it, and asked Danny to teach the occasional class on Estate Law to rookie lawyers. It was as mentor to the young and innocent that Danny gained the enduring nickname "Triple Dip."

"Never," he taught, "charge a client more than a few bucks to prepare their will. That makes them feel obligated to you enough that they won't bitch when you write yourself in as Executor. When they die, you pick up 5% of their assets as your commission. That's the first dip. The second dip is that you hire yourself, or your law partner, as the lawyer for the Estate. That's where you bang it for another 5%. And the third dip," (by now the dumbest rookie was chuckling happily and scribbling furiously in his notebook) "is that as long as you can keep the estate in your office, you can milk it for 6% of any income it earns before you let go of it. So if the guy leaves $500,000, you pick up $25,000 right off the bat as Executor, another $25,000 as the Estate's lawyer, and 6% of the dividends until the heirs scream for their money."

In those happy days the Bar Association published what was called a minimum fee schedule, on the theory that any lawyer who charged less than the minimum fee was bound to do a sloppy job. Eventually the Justice Department took the nasty position that this was old-fashioned price fixing and a criminal violation of the anti-trust laws. But until they did, it was a mark of the admiration in which his money-making talents were held by the local Bar that Triple Dip was re-appointed annually as Chair of the Minimum Fee Committee. You see today those Godawful ads for $99 divorces, but in Triple Dip's day, the minimum rate was $1,500. Plus expenses.

Continuing his life-long program of investing in politics, Triple Dip decided the time had come for his brother to run for office. The brother in question had served for thirty years as an affable if bumbling obstetrician whose chief claim to fame was staying awake while the nurses delivered the baby, and not dropping it when they handed it to him to present to the happy mother. "Little Dip", as he became known, had only to give his brother a mailing list of the proud parents whose babies he delivered during the previous 30 years, and Triple Dip did the rest. They beat the highly competent but incorrigibly corrupt incumbent in a walk, and Triple Dip was now a serious player.

Meanwhile, the Little Bo Peep Paint Company decided the paint business bored the shit out of them. So they changed the name to "Bonne Chance" and bought a smart little casino on a lovely palm-treed island where the politicians were few in number and relatively cheap in price. While profitable and more fun than stocking paint cans in hardware stores, they soon realized that the real money lay in tapping the huge reservoir of untraced cash that lay in the underground economies of New York, Philadelphia, and Washington. For this they needed a more conveniently located casino, preferably on a coastal island where the local politicians were few in number and relatively cheap in price. Atlantic City came promptly to mind and, if it had no palm trees, it more than made up for them by being so close to the mainland the teeming millions could drive over the bridges and causeways with their cash.

Casting about for a man who could deliver the legal and political goods, Bonne Chance hooked up with Triple Dip, paid him a million dollar retainer (plus expenses), and the new Atlantic City was born.

The first casino referendum had been run by urban renewal types determined to convince the public that casinos would rebuild the cities. When it crashed and burned, Triple Dip saw immediately what had gone wrong. He quickly ran up $3 million in untraceable "expenses" which bought the necessary legislative support to get the new referendum on the ballot, and insured that the newly-rich-and-hoping-to-get-richer politicians would deliver the pro-casino votes on election day. Triple Dip didn't know any more about urban renewal than he did about practicing law, but he knew how to grease the right wheels to get things moving. They didn't know it, but the days of the Skin Game were coming to an end, and Sonia's whorehouse was about to be replaced by state of the art "Escort Services for Discriminating Gentlemen."

Chapter 20

While they geared up for a new, and far better funded, referendum campaign, neither Triple Dip nor Bonne Chance were in any hurry to let it be known what they were up to locally. Bonne Chance wanted a lock on huge stretches of Atlantic City's beach-block slums before word got out and prices went up. While malleable politicians from North Jersey were given drums and bugles to lead the pro-casino parade in the populous northern counties, in Atlantic City Triple Dip and his client bought an option here, a tax-sale property there, quietly assembling large blocks of land under a confusing tangle of names. Editorials began to appear urging Atlantic City to clean up its image, and indictments of corrupt local politicians (or at least the one's who'd set their price too high) increased. But for the most part, life on the surface went on as usual. The hookers worked Pacific Avenue and the bars. "Upside Down Norma" still kept the Happy Hour crowd happy with her trapeze act at the go-go lounge. Failing businesses suffered mysterious but well-insured fires. Conventions came and went, although with decreasing oomph.

Fortunately, every city has traditions, and those of Atlantic City were strong and sensible, including the end-of-summer police crackdowns on Boardwalk hustlers – the cheap auction houses where shills jacked up bids for $50 fake Oriental rugs to $500 before letting the suckers take them for $550; the time-share hustlers who sold you free vacations in Florida if you'd agree to look at their latest development; the gypsy fortune-tellers in booth-sized shops along the Boardwalk who offered to tell you of mysterious lovers, exotic trips and fantastic riches all as described by the lines on your palm.

By general consent you could hustle, bamboozle, steal from and otherwise skin the tourists all summer long, for a modest split of the take with the cop on the beat. But come the end of season, the cops needed newspaper ink to prove they were on the job. Since Labor Day marked the end of the season and the beginning of Miss America week, what better day to bust the hustlers and gypsies, and convert the City from Baghdad-on-the-Boardwalk to Disneyland-with-Salt-Water-Taffy?

Of course, local jealousies play their role. The cops in the surrounding towns, having too little crime of their own and hungry for an occasional shot at stardom, drummed up a little action on their own from time to time. So on Labor Day, anticipating the usual gypsy raid, the mainland cops decided to join the posse. While Atlantic City's finest were busting the Boardwalk gypsies, their counterparts raided Celia's on the mainland.

To the ignorant eye, a gypsy's a gypsy, and Celia's fortune-telling was as illegal as any on the Boardwalk. There was, however, a big difference, at least in the eyes of Celia and her husband Steve.

"We're not a business!" Steve insisted. "We're a church! Our house is the only Gypsy church in existence! It's tax exempt, and they got no right to arrest us for fortune telling!"

"But Celia *is* a fortune teller," I pointed out.

"Yeah, but it ain't a business. It's a religion! She don't charge money! All we do is accept donations. They can't arrest you for practicin' religion. Not in your own church!"

He had a good point. The cops had arrested Celia based on an undercover agent who'd gone in, given Celia money, and been assured by her, with near-hypnotic intensity, that he faced great danger, would come through it safely only if he was extremely careful, and within a year would receive the good news he was hoping for. This, the prosecutor opened to the jury in a somewhat bored voice, was fortune-telling for money, a criminal violation.

"What, exactly," I asked the jury after we'd gone through the witnesses, "is the difference between what Celia told the officer, and what he could have read in the horoscope section of the Press? If you buy the newspaper to look up your horoscope, you're paying money for somebody to tell your future. But is the Press on trial here? No. All this trial is about is that the defendant's a Gypsy!"

Then, of course, I went too far. The most important part of jury work is knowing when to shut up. The jury – even Judge Horsen – were nodding in agreement. The prosecutor was squirming. But, being on a roll, I couldn't let well enough alone. I had to hammer it home.

"And this was not even a commercial transaction like buying a newspaper," I plunged on. "Celia never charges. All she asks is a voluntary donation. Their's is a church, not a business. What's the difference," I challenged, "between going to church and having the minister preach that hellfire awaits the sinful but that you'll be saved, and what Celia said?" Twelve jurors grew tense, the prosecutor frowned, and the judge looked at me like a cop watching a drunk stumble down the yellow line. He was with me intellectually, but aghast at my stupidity.

"Your Honor," the prosecutor seized the moment, "I object! I don't think the jury has to listen to any comparison between this fortune teller and the venerable teachings of the world's great religions!"

"In chambers, gentlemen," Judge Horsen ordered. "The jury will take a brief recess." As we trooped into the judge's chambers it slowly dawned on me that I should have shut my yap three sentences ago.

"Donovan, what the hell are you doing? Have you lost your mind?" The judge was not happy. His views on organized religion were skeptical to start with. His Jewish grandfather had died at Dachau with any number of Gypsies herded into Hitler's ovens. Celia's prosecution made him extremely uncomfortable, and just when he thought I was winning, he'd watched in stunned amazement as I offended the religious belief of every juror.

Sol Rivkin, an old salt of a prosecutor who's views weren't much different from the Judge's, leaned forward as I was about to defend myself. "Donovan, do yourself a favor. Just shut up and go along with this." He turned to Judge Horsen. "Dave," he said, talking to a man 3 years his junior whom he'd known for 50 years, "I don't want this. If I'd spotted it earlier, I'd have killed it in the office. I'll agree, if you dismiss the jury, to downgrade this to consumer fraud. We'll take a $50 fine and let it go."

"But Judge," I protested, "this is their religion!"

Horsen pointed his finger at me with a no-nonsense look in his eye. "Donovan, for a smart guy you can be remarkably thick! Where the hell do you think the Salem witchcraft trials came from? You think that jury's going to equate this woman with their own ministers and priests? Or that an appeal court's going to reverse on the ground that she's some kind of Gypsy pope? Now here's what's going to happen," he leaned forward. "You're going out there right now and sell your client this deal. Trust me, she'll buy it. She's no more religious than I am. But if you go back in front of that jury they'll find her guilty in a heartbeat."

I wasn't convinced I should abandon the fight for freedom of religion so easily, but Celia saw it in more practical terms. "Okay," she said, pleased, "so long as it doesn't make me close up shop." The prosecutor agreed, the deal was done, and Celia and Steve, despite all evidence to the contrary, concluded I was a helluva lawyer.

Chapter 21

I gnoring the clean image bunch who were busting their guts trying to convince upstate voters Atlantic City had cleaned up its act and could be trusted with casinos, flashes of the old Atlantic City kept fighting their way through. The schoolteacher's convention livened everybody's day when the cops took the Press along on a raid of a porno film-making operation featuring young schoolmarms in skin-flicks calculated to satisfy the horniest high school boy.

Schoolteachers weren't the only movie-makers in town. Barry Stewart announced that The Flying Cloud, a wooden replica of the famous clipper ship specially built to attract tourists for short cruises along the shore, had been chartered to a film-making company for the production of a swashbuckling pirate thriller. The Flying Cloud was Barry's brainchild. He was a man whose reputation as the best trial lawyer in town was marred only by his frequent but misguided efforts at civic improvement. Confronted by local banks who balked at lending money to Jews or Blacks, who refused to cash welfare checks and who preferred their customers to wait in hour-long lines rather than hire extra tellers, Barry put together a bunch of new investors and opened his own bank, which made money from the day it opened. If he'd stopped there, he'd have been a hero. But he kept going. Emboldened by the success of his bank, Barry indulged his boyhood dream of owning an ice hockey team, to be based in Atlantic City. Soon he was everywhere, signing up star players with multi-million dollar deals, hiring coaches, running ad campaigns, goosing the government to spruce up the ice-skating rink in Convention Hall. It went bust, of course. There's only so many hockey nuts to go around.

From there, things went downhill for Barry. When a gray-stone church across from the bank lost its congregation to the suburbs, he converted it into the "Sherwood Forest" restaurant. The bartenders wore quivers full of arrows that kept knocking over the bottles, the waitresses objected to what they called "this Maid Marion bullshit", and the *maitre d'*, already sensitive about his weight, refused to wear the Friar Tuck outfit. But what eventually killed the place was the heating bill. Churches have high ceilings, and when you redecorate them to look like castles, they still have high ceilings. Barry developed sympathy for the original Sheriff of Nottingham and his high taxes. Feeding those fireplaces was expensive.

While Barry was juggling heating bills and freezing waitresses at Sherwood Forest, running his law firm and his bank, and hustling charters for the Flying Cloud, the old YMCA across the street went belly-up, seized for failure to pay withholding taxes on the help.

"YMCA Building Goes To Bankruptcy Auction" proclaimed the caption under a front page photo of the five story brick building.

"Hey, man, we gotta talk." John Washington sounded urgent. He was a black ex-con with a clear head about what he wanted and didn't want. Right now he wanted me. Since the drug rehab program he ran was my biggest client, I went right over.

"You see this?" he asked, pointing to the Press.

"Yeah, saw it this morning."

"We gotta get it, man. They's enough room in that building we can fit in a bed for every dope fiend in town!"

John had been doing seven to ten for armed robbery, a bad-ass who stood out in the State's major league of bad-asses, when he watched a fly crawl over a pile of horse shit on the prison farm. "Fly didn't *know* his life wasn't nothin' but a pile of horse shit," John told me one night when we were deep in a bottle of wine over a chess game. "An' I wasn't no smarter than that fly – jumpin' from one pile of shit to another thinkin' I was gettin' somewhere. Doin' dope, stealin' so's I could do more dope – and spendin' half my life in prison!"

When he left prison and the horse shit behind, he rounded up five of his best buddies who were, naturally, the five biggest drug-users in town. Between them, their drug habits had caused about half of Atlantic City's crime rate. He'd been their leader before, and stayed their leader now. Only now he made them see how drugs were killing black kids. The Black Muslims were working the same side of the street, but giving up wine, women and song along with drugs was John's idea of overkill. He also thought the politics of black power got in the way of dealing with the drug problem, which was beginning to explode into the white communities downbeach. Free of distractions about religion, politics and race, John spent his days going head to head with drug addicts. He set up counseling sessions in a cheap storefront, lived off donations when and where he could get them, and wasn't bashful about asking for more.

He spoke at a Hadassah meeting, this six-foot, two-inch fierce-looking black man, and scared the hell out of the good ladies by telling them how and where their kids could buy dope, what changes of behavior they should look out for, and how to search bedrooms and bathrooms for drugs, needles, cookers, and other works. The Hadassah gave him $5,000. He put his buddies on the payroll at $40 a week and, armed with the Hadassah's membership list, hit every Jewish businessman in town with a fund-raising *tour de force* that left the United Jewish Appeal green with envy. He squeezed four beds into the back room of the storefront, got a friendly doctor to treat the addicts with methadone, put the addicts on round-the-clock work and counseling, and hit up the Episcopalians, Lutherans, Catholics, Baptists, and Methodists. By the time he called me to form a non-profit corporation for him, he'd raised enough money to rent a defunct roller-skating rink on Baltic Avenue, got the unions to donate labor and the building supply outfits to give him Sheetrock and lumber, and got Manny Gottinger to skip fishing for awhile and supervise the conversion of the skating rink into a twenty-bed methadone treatment clinic.

Manny was about 70, a blue-eyed, sunburnt, sparsely-built man who wore old khaki pants, sweaters with holes worn at the elbows and drove around town in a beat-up station wagon with his toolbox in the back. We'd hit it off immediately when we first met. For one thing, he knew his stuff. For another, he'd heard about my getting Sonia's shoebox back for her, which fit his sense of the rightness of things. As a boy, he'd run errands for Sonia back in her heyday, and she'd been a generous tipper. Plus, we shared the same dress code. I hated ties, hats, coats, and any pants with a crease in them. So'd he. On such foundations are lasting friendships built. But, like the rest of the world, I judged books by their covers, and figured him a likeable but not particularly impressive guy. Mostly retired from active building, he kept his warehouse and office more as a place to store his fishing charts and get away from the house than for real business. Most of what he earned now came from insurance appraisals, when insurance companies needed to know how much a building was going to cost to repair or replace. Aside from being honest, he thought in dollars per square foot, and knew to the penny prices on every building material known to man. He'd been born and raised in Atlantic City, growing up in a family of five children who lived over their parent's shop. The shop was run on the 10% principle: On the books every cost was shown as 10% higher than actual; every receipt 10% lower. "It avoided confusion," Manny said. "No need to keep two sets of books to know how you were doing."

As a young builder, Manny had done okay – until the day he fell in love with Jeanette Martindale, a good, Protestant girl whose family owned – I'll put this in Monopoly terms – Park Place and Boardwalk. Not literally, but you get the idea. The best schools, member of the best country clubs (no Jews, Blacks or Catholics allowed), year-long trips to Europe. She was rich, smart, beautiful, and deeply in love with a struggling Jewish contractor named Emmanuel Z. Gottingen, which had not exactly been in the family's plans for her future.

"How'd that happen?" I asked over lunch.

"Damned if I know," Manny said. "We took one look at each other and that was it. First thing I knew she was pregnant, and her family's treating me like the Anti-Christ. Mine wasn't much better, but hers were real bastards."

"Not much they could do about it," I finished the story.

"The hell they couldn't. First they put pressure on her to go to Europe for an abortion. Then they offered me $50,000 to leave town. That's when we headed for Elkton and came back married."

"So they cut her off without a dime?" I'd read all the old novels and knew how these things were handled.

"I wish the bastards had," Manny snorted. "It would've save me a hell of a lot of money. But her grandfather had set up a trust they couldn't break. So they spread it all over town I wasn't to get any contracts, told everybody I'd married her for her money, and shut me off from any bank credit so I couldn't bid on any decent jobs. I got so pissed I called up her old man and told him I wouldn't touch a dime of her money and he could shove it up his ass."

"And you never did," I finished the story again.

"Worst than that," Manny grinned. "I told him not only would we live off what I earned, but I'd pay the taxes on whatever income she got from the trust fund. I didn't know how much she got each year, or I'd have kept my mouth shut. We been married 40 years, and every year I gotta come up with half a million bucks just to pay her goddam taxes!" I don't know which emotion he felt stronger; anger at the decades-old prejudice they'd shown or triumph that he had, in fact, shoved it up their ass. "They" were mostly dead, of course, but lived vividly in Manny's memory. I figured he'd go on paying those taxes and bitching about it 'til he died. You can't help loving a man that stubborn.

John Washington had pulled Manny into supervising the remake of the skating rink to a methadone clinic before he knew what was happening. "The son of a bitch even got me working with those union bastards," Manny groused. "Swore I'd never do it, but all of Jeanette's friends are in that goddam Hadassah and it got so we couldn't go out to dinner without her and her friends bendin' my ear. Then this sneaky son of a bitch," he glared at John, "put Jeanette on his board of directors." John grinned, entirely unashamed of such manipulation.

The politicians were next. John soon learned the art of leveraging matching funds. Get $10,000 from the City and that's the 10% match you need to get another $90,000 from the state. We took that $100,000 and landed a federal grant of $1.5 million. Reading the fine print in the grant papers, I found a neat little paragraph about an indirect cost rate, which is how the Pentagon pays the overhead run up by defense contractors. Turned out the same system applied to us. I negotiated an overhead rate of 47%, which jacked our total take up to about $2.25 million a year, each year for the next five years.

It was about a week after we'd landed that federal whale that the YMCA went on the auction block. The 20 bed skating rink was already up to 30 beds and groaning at the seams. John looked at the Press picture of that beautiful, five-story building complete with individual bedrooms, showers, indoor basketball court, swimming pool and office space like a kid opening a Christmas present.

"That place is run down and needs work," I said. "Manny's gonna shit. We only got this place done three months ago."

John laughed. "He'll go along. I'm makin' Jeannette President of the Board. 'Sides, he don't know it yet, but she sent us a check for $25,000. Said Manny needed the tax deduction." He studied the picture again. "Oh, man! We gotta get that motha! Gimme that buildin' an' there won't be a dope fiend left! How we gonna do it?"

The following week I was in the front row at bankruptcy court when the Y went up for sale. The minimum bid had been set at $110,000, and I had a certified check in my pocket for just that amount. The courtroom was filled with the usual bankruptcy lawyers and real estate bottom – fishers, but the Y wasn't on anybody else's wish list. It was too far uptown for the convention trade, and Triple Dip and Bonne Chance were busy putting together a block they'd need for their casino's parking garage when the referendum passed. Truth was, the YMCA was just another old derelict drifting in the Sargasso Sea we called Atlantic City. I bid $110,000 in my own name "or my nominee". The hammer fell and I presented the $110,000 check to the judge. As the Press reported next day, John Washington and his recovering drug addicts were about to move from Baltic Avenue to Pacific; the kind of move Monopoly players pray for and the Chamber of Commerce shudders to think about.

Barry Stewart, never a racist but certain that neither Pacific Avenue nor his bank nor the shaky Sherwood Forest restaurant could survive an onslaught of drug addicts, panicked. Too smart to be his own lawyer, he called in the heavy artillery.

"Donovan, this is your telephone notice. I'm going before Judge Goldberg two o'clock this afternoon for an order setting that bankruptcy sale aside."

"Norman! What the hell are you doing?" I was incredulous. Norman Kartman was the heaviest legal cannon in the state; a decorated Marine Corps officer, advisor to the Israeli military and combative trial lawyer. Getting hit by Norman was like driving a Volkswagen into the path of an oncoming steamroller.

"I'm representing Sherwood Forest, and the Bank," Norman answered.

"I don't give a damn if you're representing the Pope," I said. "The hammer fell! Once the hammer falls at a bankruptcy auction, the sale's final. You know that as well as I do!"

"Not if the sale wasn't properly advertised," Norman shot back. "Nobody got proper notice. That's why there weren't any other bidders. Once casinos get here, that property's gonna be valuable. I'll be there at 2 o'clock asking the Judge to re-open the sale, and I'll have a certified check for $165,000 to start the bidding."

John Washington took the news with more calm than I did. "Fuck him. They wanna bid, we'll outbid 'em. Let's show up with a certified check for $175,000!"

I threw up my hands. "We can't do it, John! We're not up against some real estate developer. We're bidding against Barry Stewart's fuckin' bank, and Barry's got a hard on for us. How far you think our money's gonna go?"

"Then we gonna find out if that law degree you got's any good," John said grimly.

In Court I raised all the hell I could, but the Bankruptcy Judge, Bill

Goldberg, had been appointed to the job by Franklin Delano Roosevelt the year I was born, was the senior bankruptcy judge in the country, and was fully capable of balancing the finality of a bankruptcy sale against the chance of getting another $50,000 back for the creditors. He "took the matter under advisement", ordered us to submit briefs on just how final a bankruptcy sale really is, and scheduled a hearing to take testimony as to whether the sale had been adequately advertised.

Chapter 22

The call came a short month after Judge Horsen and Solly Rivkin had kept me out of trouble in the gypsy fortune-telling case.

"Donovan! It's me! Steve! We had a fire! Can you handle the insurance claim?"

"Yeah, sure," I said. "Anybody hurt? Celia okay?"

"Yeah, yeah, she's fine," Steve said. "But we lost a lot of stuff. Must be a hundred thousand dollars of stuff got burned. Rugs, meat in the freezer, paintings, furniture. And the house! Half of it's burned to the frame."

"How much insurance do you have?"

"We had $50,000 on the house and $30,000 on the contents, but we just increased it to $100,000 on the contents and $125,000 on the building."

"When? When did you jack up the insurance?" Fires that happen right after the insurance is increased draw arson investigators like flowers draw bees.

"Just last week. Thank God, Celia had a premonition! The new policy came in the mail the morning of the fire! Will you help us?"

A premonition? Wonderful. Suddenly I had a premonition of my own. Visions of jail rose before me. I could see pictures of myself, handcuffed to Steve and Celia, being led off to prison over the caption "Gypsy Arsonists and Crooked Lawyer Convicted of Defrauding Insurance Company," with a subheading: "Increased Insurance Based on 'Premonition', Insists Fortune Teller Who Recently Pleaded Guilty to Consumer Fraud!"

Expecting the worst, I called Jack Jenner, the motorcycle cop from the Skin Game. It wasn't his turf, but cops in one town always have contacts in others. He called the county arson team for me. "Say's they're clean," Jack called back that same day. "Some drunk fell asleep under their back porch smoking a cigarette. No evidence of arson."

"Thanks, Jack. I owe you."

"Nah. Might need you myself someday." Jack understood the perils of the practicing lawyer and of honest cops. Either of us could get in the wrong crosshairs any given day.

Assured Steve and Celia hadn't set the fire themselves, my next step was making sure the damage claimed was legit.

"Bills of Sale? For what?" Steve was not a man to ask for or hang on to Bills of Sale.

"Well, that $15,000 Oriental rug, for example. What proof do we have that's what you paid for it, and that it's genuine?"

"We didn't pay for it! It was a donation to the church. But don't worry. I can get a letter from the people that donated it. They're Gypsies. They'll understand."

Yeah, I thought. I'm going to fight the insurance company armed with sworn affidavits from people with changeable names and no fixed addresses.

"Steve, I'm going to hire some appraisers. One for the building damage, and one for the personal property. When they come, show them everything, and answer every question."

I had Manny appraise the building damage. To get the contents appraised, I tracked down an estate appraiser from mainline Philadelphia; a guy whose impeccable credentials would, I hoped, keep me out of jail. A few weeks went by before he called.

"Mr. Donovan," he called, "I've sent you my appraisal and my bill in the mail."

"How'd it go?" I asked, dreading news that Steve and Celia's stuff had been grossly over-valued in their claim.

"Oh, there's no question. The contents were of exceptional quality and quite genuine. From the remnants of the Oriental rug, I was able to verify it as a genuine Sarouk. It was worth at least $20,000, possibly $25,000. Pity, really. Quite beautiful."

"And the rest?"

"Well, that's why I called you." My heart sank. "I understand they had $100,000 coverage on the contents?"

"Yes," I replied cautiously.

"Well, when you get my report, you'll see I had no trouble appraising their loss well in excess of $100,000. They should be able to collect the full amount."

"You're kidding!" If we could get $100,000 on the contents and the full $125,000 Manny had estimated on the building repairs, my 10% fee would fill a lot of potholes on my financial highway.

"Well," the dry voice of the appraiser continued, "I didn't want to put this in writing, but I thought you should know that your client offered me $5,000 if I'd inflate the appraisal. And that was *after* I'd already told him the damages far exceeded his coverage. Very strange. But I thought you'd want to know."

"Yeah, I guess so. Thanks," I said weakly.

"Don't worry about it," Manny said when I told him. "He offered me the same thing."

"But why?" I was dumbfounded. "Why offer a guy a bribe when he's already told you that you're in good shape?"

"Makes sense," Manny grinned. "The insurance company's gonna send in their own appraiser, who's gonna lowball it. You'll end up splittin' the difference. All Steve's doing is trying to jack up the high end as far as he can. Happens all the time." Try finding that bit of learning in law school!

I survived Celia's premonitions and Steve's shenanigans, got the money, paid a bunch of bills, and swore off Gypsies, fortune tellers, and any insurance case based on premonitions. I went back to work on the YMCA case. Triple Dip had been thinking things over, and decided to throw his weight behind Barry. Suddenly the newspapers began editorializing about how inappropriate it was, just when the City was on the verge of getting casinos, to see its prestigious Pacific Avenue filled with drug addicts who could surely be treated in suitable facilities elsewhere.

Chapter 23

I was up to my eyeballs in research on bankruptcy law when Kathy Walton called. It was one of those tearful calls from a distraught mother nobody turns down. Kathy and Bobby were good people; hardworking and blessed with a marvelous son, Billy, whose only limitation was that he'd been born without arms. Billy didn't realize for his first four or five years that he'd been born without arms, and by that time his balance was perfect, he used his feet for hands, and he could run, jump, and get in mischief with the best of them.

By the time he started school all the kids in the neighborhood knew him, had played with him, and forgotten there was any difference between themselves and him. He played street hockey with the same energy and aggressiveness his uncles and cousins had, and was always one of the first kids picked when kids chose up sides.

When he finished sixth grade, he moved from his neighborhood school to junior high, where a new Principal decided there was a real danger of the school being sued if Billy lost his balance and fell off his chair. He insisted that, to be safe, Billy had to wear a helmet in class. That lasted about an hour of the first day, and ended when an eighth-grader taunted Billy in the hall with "Helmet Head!"

By the time the teachers regained control, Billy had kicked the kid in the ribs, butted him in the head, and had him pinned to the wall with a foot to his throat. The Principal promptly suspended Billy and informed his parents Billy should be sent off to a special school "for emotionally troubled students."

I knew the YMCA was important, but I wasn't about to let Billy down. Fortunately, I was able to get a quick hearing scheduled before an Administrative Law Judge, a bureaucrat in black robes whose career depended on how well he looked after his fellow bureaucrats, such as school Principals.

The hearing began badly. The Principal testified about the effect of armless children on school insurance premiums if they fell out of chairs; the teacher testified about the mayhem in the hallway; and the other kid's parents testified about the physical and psychological trauma their little darling had suffered at the hands – or feet – of the "emotionally disturbed" Billy. Neither they nor the Judge agreed that being called "Helmet Head" would get anybody's blood up.

I decided outside help was needed, and spent the evening arranging it.

When we picked it up next morning it was my turn to put on witnesses. I called up Billy, who was polite enough but gave the general impression he'd just as soon jam a foot into the Judge's throat as put up with any order sending him away from home. Billy's parents, uncles and cousins were equally polite, but one got the flavor of American farmers testifying before one of George III's royal judges and considering whether to answer his questions or take him out and hang him. The Waltons, active, hardworking and energetic, did not come from submissive stock.

I put on Billy's hockey coach – a 20 year veteran of the State Troopers who gave it as his opinion that Billy was as physically tough and emotionally stable as any boy he'd ever known. That pushed the Judge back some, but not enough. He looked at his watch, gauging whether he could get his findings and decision on the record before lunch. "Gentlemen, if you'd please approach the bench." We moved up as he leaned over, putting his hand on the mike. "Mr. Donovan, do you have any further witnesses?" He eyed the two figures in the back of the room.

"No, sir," I answered.

"And you, counselor?" he asked the School Board's lawyer.

"No, sir."

"Hmmn. I see two people back there and wondered if either of you know – ?" His bureaucratic antennae were alert.

"No idea who they are," answered my adversary. The Judge looked at me inquisitively. He wasn't sure what it was, but he sensed something nasty coming his way.

"Actually, your Honor," I put on the most innocent face I'd managed since getting thrown off the Alter Boys at Holy Spirit grade school, "I think they're from the Press."

"The Press?" The judicial angst was sudden and strong.

"Yessir. The woman's a reporter and I think her companion's a photographer. Their editor seems to think this would make a great story." I felt it irrelevant to add that he began to think so after I'd poured six beers down his throat the night before.

"The Press!" The Judge's mournful whisper was music to my ears. "I wonder why they're here?"

"I think the boy's uncle is one of the printers in the pressroom," I said. Truthful enough, if a bit incomplete. Billy's uncle was the Press's shop steward, and the editor had gotten the word, even through the six beers, that favorable coverage of Billy's plight might ease management-labor relations considerably.

"You son of a bitch! You set this up!" the School Board's lawyer growled.

"Prove it," I shot back, as a very worried Administrative Law Judge shuffled his papers and envisioned tomorrow's headlines.

"Counselor," he eyed the School Board's lawyer with the look of a man determined not to be tomorrow's newspaper roadkill, "off the record, it seems to me there's no reason a boy who can play hockey as well as that State Trooper testified should be made to wear a helmet. Why don't we take a short recess so you can work something out with Mr. Donovan?"

What we worked out was an agreement that Billy did *not* have to wear a helmet unless and until he actually fell off his chair and got hurt

– after which, if he was seriously injured, he'd wear a helmet. Try explaining that logic to a 6ᵗʰ grader.

We went out to lunch; Billy, his parents, me, the reporter and the photographer. After lunch we got some kids together on a sand dune playing King of the Hill which produced, next day, a Press caption "No Helmet for Billy!" under a picture showing the armless and triumphant Billy cheerfully rolling his playmates down the hill with his feet.

Chapter 24

"You can't hurt Joe Snyder," Manny insisted.

"Manny, he got on the stand and testified that he appraised the YMCA at $165,000! What am I supposed to do? Lie down and let Norman wipe up the floor with me?"

"All I'm tellin' you is you can't hurt Joe Snyder. The Judge is Bill Goldberg, and his sister Rose and Joe used to go together."

"Manny, that was fifty goddam years ago! And they never got married!"

"No, but Goldberg likes Joe, and now that Rose is dead and Joe's wife just died, he feels sorry for him. You make Joe Snyder look foolish, and Bill Goldberg's gonna nail you to the wall."

Law in Atlantic City had nothing to do with facts or precedents. It operated based on the ghosts of long-dead friends and enemies. We'd done the briefs on the finality of Bankruptcy sales, and started the hearing as to whether the sale of the YMCA had been adequately advertised. Norman had started the day by hauling out his $165,000 check, then put real estate appraiser Joe Snyder on the stand. Joe, in his eighties, courtly, gentle, experienced to the point of senility, and beloved by all, had spend the afternoon testifying that he'd appraised the building, and that it was clearly worth well in excess of our $110,000 – in fact, it was worth at least the $165,000 newly offered by Barry Stewart's bank.

Like everybody who ate lunch at the Stanley or got their hair cut at Angelo's, I knew and liked old Joe Snyder. The death of his wife of 50 years a month earlier had left him devastated but gamely going through the motions of a life emptied of her presence. Putting on white shirt, neat tie, and respectable suit and doddering around town doing the occasional appraisal was all that was holding him together emotionally. We were all rooting for him.

On cross-examination, I'd been sure that Joe's had been a "windshield appraisal," in which he stayed in the car, relying on his experience and memory to come up with a value for the building he'd probably examined a dozen times over the years. Probing for a flaw in the appraisal, I asked him how high the building was.

"Five stories," he answered, accurately enough.

"And wouldn't you say, based on your experience, that a building that high is worth a great deal less if it has no elevator?"

"Oh, certainly. But it has an elevator."

There it was, dropped into my lap. I'd been all over that building, and climbed every one of the five flights of stairs to the top. There was no elevator, and never had been. I could take Joe's appraisal apart in an instant, but first I had to nail down that he hadn't just made a simple mistake in his statement. Getting a witness to confirm his own mistake is tricky business. If you ask them the same question twice, they realize something's up and, if they don't, their lawyer does. So I slid around the question as to whether the place had an elevator.

"Do you remember which side of the building that elevator's on?" I asked instead.

"On the right, I think. Yes, on the right as you go in." Joe was polite but firm, far out on the treacherously thin ice of memory.

"You're sure?"

"Oh, yes. In fact, I rode up in it." Fifty years of appraisals, thousands of buildings, too many memories, too many years, and too much grief had led this gentle old soul into the quicksand. I didn't like doing it, but unless I discredited his appraisal, we'd lose the case and the building. I was debating how best to blow his testimony apart when the Judge, glancing at the clock, announced it was four o'clock and ordered a recess until 9 A.M.

Over dinner Manny, who knew as well as I did the Y had no elevator, told me the facts of life about a love that had bloomed and died long before I was born.

"You just can't hurt Joe Snyder," Manny repeated. "You do that and he'll never get another appraisal in this town. He'll be dead in a month and you'll never be able to live with yourself."

"I don't want to," I said, "but I can't let that elevator go unchallenged. It affects the whole case."

"I wouldn't touch it with a ten foot pole," Manny looked at me steadily. "If you put me on that stand and ask me about an elevator, I'll swear I didn't notice."

Norman, of all people, saved the situation. He called me at home that night to inform me he'd gotten the Judge to grant a delay of the next morning's start from 9 AM until 10 AM.

"Okay by me, but why the delay?"

"Joe Snyder's wife died last month. He goes to synagogue every morning."

"Thanks, Norman." I hesitated. Then Manny's advice and my conscience kicked in together and I did the right thing. "Call him back and tell him while he's there he should say one more prayer."

"For you?"

"Nah. For an elevator."

"There's no elevator? Damn! I knew you were on to something!"

"Look, Norm. I can't hurt the old guy. How about I yield to you in the morning and you get him to correct his testimony?"

"Well, you're probably the son of a bitch Barry says you are, but at least you're a *mensch*. All right. I'll straighten it out. And I owe you one."

"You did the right thing," Manny said next morning as Joe got off the stand.

"Yeah. Now all I've gotta do is cross-examine a trial lawyer who was cross-examining witnesses when I was still in short pants," I muttered as Norman called Barry Stewart to the stand.

Chapter 25

Barry's testimony was straightforward and impressive. Norman brought it out with just the right touch. Here was this distinguished lawyer; a leading businessman, banker, restaurant owner and civic leader all rolled up into one, testifying in the clearest terms that the sale of the YMCA had been so poorly advertised that even he hadn't heard about it until the sale was over. If he had, he'd have been there ready to buy that valuable property – and was ready, willing and able to top our price by $55,000 – and more, if necessary. He testified he was also active in the drive to get casinos approved, and believed that an "inappropriate" use of the YMCA would hurt the cause.

I admired Barry, but he was no Joe Snyder. I started out with brass knuckles and piled on from there.

"Mr. Stewart," I asked, "you own a law firm, a restaurant and a bank, right?"

"I've been lucky," he answered modestly.

"And do you visit all three places every day?"

"I don't understand what relevance that has," he answered, good trial lawyer that he was. Unfortunately for him, he wasn't there as a lawyer but as a witness, which is the difference between showing up at a duck hunt as the hunter, or as the duck

"Let's leave questions of relevance to counsel and the Judge, shall we? Just answer the question," I put a truly nasty patronizing spin into my voice. Barry reacted like a man stung by a bee. All his trial-lawyer aggression came to the fore.

"What's your question got to do with anything?" he demanded.

"Your Honor, I ask this witness be directed to answer the question." I pushed right back.

Judge Goldberg, who'd seen me ease off on Joe Snyder, and appreciated it, gave me the break I needed. "The witness knows better than to argue with counsel," he said, not bothering to look at Barry. "Answer the question." Now, instead of a calm, competent professional fielding my questions, I had a seething-mad hostile witness aching for revenge, and certain he could outsmart me. Nothing helps a cross-examination more than an angry witness with a big ego.

"Yes. Unless I'm in trial, I'm in the law office."

"And you visit your bank and your restaurant every day?"

"Yes."

"How do you get from the office to the bank or restaurant?"

"I walk. It's only three blocks. I go up South Carolina to Pacific, then down Pacific."

"So you walk right by the YMCA? Almost every day?"

"Of course."

I turned to First Count, who ducked into the hallway and brought in a large poster board on which I had mounted a blown-up photograph of a posted notice, taped to the front door of the Y, which announced in three-inch high letters: "Bankruptcy Sale!" followed by smaller print giving dates and details.

"And did you see this notice on your daily walk?" Barry's face got red. "You did see it, didn't you?" I persisted.

"I must have seen it. But I probably assumed it was a notice of closing. I never read it."

"It was a legal notice but you, a lawyer, never read it?"

"Your Honor, counsel's bullying the witness!" Norman objected. The courtroom, filled with locals who knew all the players, broke out in chuckles. Judge Goldberg stayed on my side. "This witness has been a trial lawyer for 25 years," he noted. "I doubt he's intimidated. Mr. Stewart, do you feel Mr. Donovan is bullying you?"

Barry turned bright scarlet. "No, Sir," he answered, using all his will power to avoid grinding his teeth.

"Then answer the question," I twisted the knife. "Did you, a lawyer, read that legal notice?"

"No. I never read it."

"Mr. Stewart, you're deeply involved in civic affairs, are you not?"

"I don't see how that's – yes, I am."

"And you're actively concerned about the decline of Atlantic City, aren't you?"

"That's why I'm here," Barry tried regaining the high ground.

"That's not entirely true is it? Actually, you're here because you claim you didn't know the Y was for sale, isn't that right?"

"It wasn't advertised."

"There was a legal notice on the door that you passed almost every day but never read, and three paid legal notices in the newspaper announcing the sale, but you claim it wasn't sufficiently advertised?"

"Not for a property like that. It should have been promoted."

"You mean it should have received more publicity?

"Much more."

"You were not aware, then, that the sale of the Y was a major news story that ran on all the local radio and television news?"

"No, I wasn't." Barry was starting to squirm. He knew enough to sense trouble coming.

"Let's play the clips and see if that refreshes your memory," I suggested. Barry glowered in silence as we played the taped news clips of various radio personalities announced the pending bankruptcy sale of the Y – and glowered even more as three different clips were run from local TV news shows.

"And you neither heard nor saw any of these? Not the notice on the door, not the legal ads in the newspaper, not the radio news, not the TV news?"

"I'm a very busy man. I didn't see any of that." Barry was on thin ice in the middle of the pond, and figured it was less dangerous to plunge ahead than to backtrack.

"One wonders what it takes to get your attention," I commented, signaling First Count to bring in the next poster board – this one covered with cloth awaiting the right moment to unveil it. "Tell me, Mr. Stewart, are you involved with the replica of the Flying Cloud that's docked in the Inlet?"

"Yes." Barry wasn't about to argue about relevancy and get slapped down again.

"And you are active in promoting its success – in getting groups to charter it, for example?"

"Certainly."

The Flying Cloud had been chartered by a film company to make what was billed as "a swashbuckling pirate adventure movie." What hadn't been advertised, until the Press broke the story, was that the pirates spent most of their time undressing, seducing, and ravishing their beautiful female captives – who, in turn, ended up controlling the ship by seducing, undressing, and otherwise pre-occupying the crew. The story of the porno film had taken up half the front page of the Press – complete with angry quotes from an embarrassed Barry Stewart, Chairman of the Flying Cloud Foundation, that he'd been lied to, that no one knew the ship was to star in a porno flick, and that once he'd been so informed by the Press, he was immediately canceling the charter.

"Tell us, Mr. Stewart," I unveiled the huge blow-up I'd had made of the front page of The Press, "did you notice this story of the film company that chartered the Flying Cloud to make a pornographic film?"

Barry went ballistic. "You son of a bitch! I had nothing to do with that!" The judge reached for his gavel. "I didn't have one damned thing to do with those sleazeballs!"

"Nobody said you did," I pointed out smoothly. "All I asked was whether you saw the picture of the Flying Cloud that ran in the Press, and read the story in which you were quoted?"

"Of course I did!" Barry was hot enough to sizzle.

"You had this newspaper – this very page – in your hands?" I persisted.

"Yes. Certainly!" he was still too hot to see the obvious. Because there, right next to the picture and the story of the lusty pirates and their willing captives, was the picture of the YMCA and its caption: "YMCA Building Goes to Bankruptcy Auction!" By his own admission, Barry had held that newspage, including the story announcing the sale, in his own hands. The courtroom broke out in laughter.

Norman didn't even try to salvage anything from the wreck. He got Barry off the stand before things got worse. Manny testified the building wasn't worth a dime more than we'd paid for it; Judge Goldberg upheld the sale; and Barry left the courtroom still muttering about what a son of a bitch I was, to the general merriment of the crowd.

Chapter 26

We nailed down the YMCA just in time. Under Triple Dip's expert guidance, the casino referendum sailed through. From then on, the approach of casinos resembled what the Indians must have felt at the coming of the railroads. Every real estate appraisal in town instantly became obsolete. The speculators arrived in platoons, driving up the price of everything in sight. Slum houses people abandoned a year earlier rather than pay $2,000 in taxes were suddenly going for $60,000, $70,000, and $80,000.

The landlord-tenant court got busy in a hurry. Landlords who'd milked their slum housing for years, squeezing rents out of the poor for leaky, cockroach-infested, unsafe housing were eager to cash in on their good luck. This they did by jacking up the rent and decreasing whatever maintenance existed. They didn't want the higher rents: What they wanted was empty housing to sell to the speculators. Old folks struggling to pay for their rent, food and medicine out of their Social Security checks got notices their rent was doubling next month.

Doing his bit to help the screwed get unscrewed, First Count brought in Julia, daughter of one of his lady friends. She could've been his daughter too, for all I know. First Count had put his shoes under a lot of beds over the years. What amazed me was that he was still welcomed by every lady friend he'd ever had. To them, he was definitely "Baby."

Julia, a single mother of two small boys, worked as a licensed practical nurse, earning just enough to qualify for a government subsidized townhouse in a relatively new project down by the Inlet. From the outside, garden-style townhouses. From the inside, a long list of bad news. Two hundred families lived in her project, which was built by Jack Suchin. Jack's father had built a successful real estate business by means of installment sales. When most folks buy a house, they borrow money from the bank. The bank holds a mortgage but you get a deed proving you own the house. Title belongs to you from the beginning. With installment sales, you don't get title to your house until you've paid every last cent for it. If the developer's corporation goes bankrupt during the 20 or 30 years it takes you to pay that last cent, your house counts as one of his assets. It goes up for auction and whatever money you paid the corporation before it went bust is gone.

Jack's old man pyramided the installment sales, using the houses, which were still in his corporation's name, as collateral for bigger and better things. After he bled the development company dry, it filed for bankruptcy. A hell of a lot of people, almost all of them black, lost houses on which they'd made payments for years. It was a skin game that made Big Dingy and Celia the Gypsy look like pikers.

Jack, following in his father's footsteps, built subsidized housing using federal loans made available on condition that he manage the housing and charge only "prevailing rents comparable to other rents in the community." The feds paid half the rent; the tenants the other half.

Like many government efforts to do good, the plan assumed that human nature had improved. It hadn't. Jack's idea of how to build subsidized housing was to keep a selection of beautiful Washington hookers on his payroll as consultants, then stage occasional seminars in the Virgin Islands for the government bureaucrats in charge of financing his projects. They were flown down to St. Thomas in Jack's leased jet, stayed in Jack's leased villa overlooking Charlotte Amalie, and were serviced by Jack's leased hookers; all cheerfully approved by the feds as the marketing and training part of Jack's overhead costs.

He had the right formula. With such easy government financing, he built more and more housing, of poorer and poorer quality. Where the Building Code called for four-inch drains, Jack used two-inch and bribed the building inspectors to look the other way. Thermostats seldom worked. On the coldest days the tenants had to choose between keeping their windows open to let the heat out, or watching their babies try to sleep in 85-degree rooms because the radiator valves were defective and there was no way to turn down the heat. Since Jack recovered the cost of utilities, plus a markup from the feds, the more heat the tenants pushed out the windows, the richer he got.

When the casino land rush began, Jack couldn't figure out a way to sell the housing that had been paid for by government funds. But recalling the "prevailing rents" clause in his federal contracts, he blew a kiss to the landlords who were doubling rents all over town, and promptly doubled his own. The feds still paid half, but so did the tenants. They screamed.

Anxious to cash in on the approval of the casino referendum at November's election, Jack wasted no time sending out notices of the coming rent increase. The notice arrived Thanksgiving week, on the same day Julia returned from her job at the nursing home and found human waste had backed up in the narrow drains and floated up in the dishwater in her kitchen sink. Enraged, she got together with her neighbors to compare notes. All had serious complaints of backed-up sewage, broken radiator valves, hazardous wiring, sagging windows, drafty doors and, the last straw, the doubling of their rent. One thing led to another, the other was First Count, and I found myself representing a full blown rent strike. Two hundred tenants started paying their rent into a trust fund I set up. Jack sent his lawyer to the landlord-tenant court in search of an order to turn over the money, and to evict all 200 families.

Unfortunately for Jack, the landlord-tenant Judge was Dave Epstein who, Jewish name notwithstanding, was the first black judge named to the bench in Atlantic County. In those civilized days when there were only 30 or so active lawyers in the county, instead of the battalions that now infest the city, the custom of the various courts was to meet in the judge's chambers before court began so we could work out which cases could go first, which could be settled with an off-the-record word from the judge, and which would need more time to take testimony. Jack's lawyer, an out-of-towner from Camden named Leo Bernstein, was late. As we sat in chambers working out settlements, the phone buzzed. The judge punched a button, and his secretary announced over the speaker phone that Mr. Bernstein was on the line. Another button, and a voice tentatively inquired if this was Judge Epstein.

"Yes, go ahead," the judge directed the speaker phone, motioning us to quiet down.

"Judge, this is Leo Bernstein," came a worried voice. "I've that rent-strike case before you this morning but I've been delayed. I wondered if it could be possible to defer that until this afternoon?" The judge glanced at me. I shrugged, and he answered "Sure. Mr. Donovan's here and has no objection. Two o'clock."

The relief in Bernstein's voice was considerable. "Thanks, Judge. I got stuck with a *pro bono* case and my client didn't show up here until five minutes ago. You know how these *schwartzas* are." Sam my rabbi was among the small crowd in chambers. At the word *schwartzas*, a contemptuous Yiddish word for blacks, Sam winced and raised his eyes to the ceiling. The rest of the crowd, all lawyers who had a high regard for Dave Epstein, looked at the speaker phone as if it had given birth to a snake.

"Sure. I understand how *schwartzas* are," the judge answered, giving us a grin, "I'll see you at two o'clock."

At two, Sam and I were standing by the courtroom door. A well-dressed, impressive – looking stranger complete with fur-collared overcoat, leather gloves, hat and expensive briefcase came to the door. He peeked in, saw a black judge sitting on the bench, and turned to us.

"Excuse me, I'm looking for Judge Epstein's courtroom," he said. Sam, enjoying the moment hugely, motioned with his thumb toward the door. With consternation, the out-of-towner peeked in again. His face turned pale.

"Judge *David Epstein?*" he asked. Sam nodded again. As the man pushed open the door with a dismayed look, Sam glanced at me with a mischievous grin, shrugged his shoulders in amusement, and took me by the arm through the door so we wouldn't miss the show.

I'll give Bernstein credit. He squared his shoulders, stuck out his chin, and walked what he thought would be his last mile. "Your Honor," he faced the judge and announced in a voice only slightly shaky, "I'm Leo Bernstein, and I think I'm in serious trouble with this Court!" Good try. The lawyers chuckled. The judge didn't.

"Oh, really?" Dave looked at him straight-faced. "What makes you think so?"

Bernstein looked around at a courtroom packed with angry black tenants. He was in an interesting dilemma. How do you word an apology to a black judge for using a term offensive to all black people without letting the room full of black people know what you're talking about? Dave didn't exactly cut his throat, but neither did he let him off the hook.

"Judge, I'm afraid I used a term this morning that might have offended – "

"*Might* have offended?" Dave asked in a mild tone.

"Surely offended," Bernstein corrected. "Unintentionally, of course."

"Unintentionally? Under what circumstances could that term not be offensive? Or do you mean you used it in your ignorance?"

"Yes, sir. Entirely. I apologize for my ignorance."

"Ignorance the term was offensive, or that you were using it to me?" Dave was deceptively low-keyed, like a psychiatrist nudging a deluded man into facing reality. Bernstein's brow glistened with sweat. The crowd fell silent. Whatever was going on, they knew what it was like for somebody to have you by the balls. Only this time the guy sweating was the white guy and the guy playing with him like a cat with a mouse was black. Whatever was going on, it was obviously a good thing. Sam's shoulders shook with suppressed mirth.

Chapter 27

Only after his sixth or seventh stammered apology was finally accepted by the judge with a wry glimmer of amusement did Bernstein realize he'd climbed frantically out of the fire only to find himself back in the frying pan. Asking any judge to evict 200 families a few weeks before Christmas was no easy job. Asking this judge to evict 200 black families with that crack about *schwartzas* still buzzing in his ear was sky-diving without a parachute. Having no choice, he plowed ahead, asking for the evictions. The courtroom, packed to the walls with hostile tenants, erupted with indignation at his request.

While Bernstein made his arguments, First Count slipped into the seat next to me at the counsel table. I'd asked him to double-check that everybody had paid their rent into my account. Having all the rent in hand is the key to a rent strike. There's the risk the landlord can get a court to order you to turn it over, but it eases relations with the judge when you can assure him you have the money and will do as ordered. Once he's satisfied you're not jerking his chain, he's a lot more willing to consider the tenants' problems. There'd been one or two stragglers, but First Count had the final money orders in his hand.

"That's all of them?" I asked.

First Count nodded. "I got Joe Parsons to talk to the last holdout. Got the money right here."

After Julia had pleaded that she was too busy with work and the kids, Joe Parsons and his wife Cynthia had been elected leaders of the rent-strikers. They were as completely opposite as Jack Spratt who ate no fat and his wife who ate no lean. Joe was an easy-going guy about six feet three inches tall, with a rangy build. His job was riding on the back of the trash truck, jumping down, lifting the trash barrels into the compactor, then swinging back aboard 'till the next stop. At day's end he came home, took a long, hot shower, opened a bottle of wine, chose from the finest jazz collection in Atlantic City, lit a joint, and leaned back to listen to music and think about fishing. In summer he'd get up after an hour or so and walk across the street to fish from the bulkhead, wine and marijuana by his side. Whatever he caught was dinner, fresh from the water, which Cynthia cooked with flair and perfect timing. Cynthia, a vigorous, laughing woman, outweighed Joe about three to one and was as hard-charging as Joe was laid-back.

Well, laid back in most things. Except when it came to collecting rent. Leaving aside technical quibbling about whether they qualified as low-income tenants in the townhouse project, Joe and Cynthia owned two old row-houses in mid-town, on which all rent was paid in cash. When it came to collecting rent, Joe focused pretty well. Other than that, he stayed loose.

After Bernstein made his pitch for the money and the evictions, I wasted no time getting it on the record that all the rent had been collected, was safe in my hands, and offered, if the judge so ordered, to turn it over on the spot. Bernstein looked relieved, until he noticed the effect my tactics had on the judge. A judge's posture can tell you a lot about how things are going. Once convinced the tenants were acting in good faith, Dave visibly relaxed and leaned back to listen to my arguments. I gave him a quick synopsis, starting with the sagging windows, moving on to the extreme and unhealthy heat and the shabby wiring, and piling it on when I got to the sewage backing up into the kitchen sink. By the time we got to that kitchen sink, with constant "Amen's" coming from the crowd, the judge was leaning forward to make his notes.

"Mr. Bernstein?" he raised his eyebrows when I'd finished.

"Your Honor, I've never heard such nonsense! There's no physical way such a thing could happen! There are traps and all sorts of safeguards built into every plumbing system to prevent just such occurrences! What happened here could only have been some kind of vegetative matter that backed up, probably from letting something go down the drain that should have gone into the trash can!"

"He sayin' I don't know shit when I'm lookin' at it?" an angry mother called out. A chorus of irate tenants joined in her comments until the judge rapped his gavel for order.

I'd come equipped with affidavits from most of the tenants, which gave the judge enough preliminary proof to hold things over for a while. As is so often the case, the money in the bank decided the outcome. The judge ordered me to hold on to it until further notice, and scheduled an expedited hearing on the condition of the various tenant homes.

"Manny," I was learning how valuable the tough old buzzard was. "I need some experts." I explained the situation, and the lawyer's insistence that it was impossible for sewage to back up into a kitchen sink.

"The hell it can't," Manny snorted. "If Jack Suchin built it, I'll bet every system he put in is below Code!" He rounded up three old buddies – his old subcontractors for plumbing and heating, electricity and windows. After they'd examined, measured, and tested every home in the project, I went back to court loaded for bear.

To save time we limited the tenant testimony to a representative sample; 10 of the worst cases. The tenants testified, the plumber testified, the electrician testified, and the window guy testified. The judge, with a delighted grin, referred the Building Code violations to the prosecutor for further investigation. Meanwhile, he ordered everything repaired, forbade any increase in the rent and instead ordered a reduction of 15% of the rent for the next two years, and a refund of one-half the rent I was holding in my trust fund.

Joe Parsons and I delivered the refund checks to the tenants at a special Christmas party the day before Christmas Eve – a blow-out unmatched before or since. At least, that part of it I was able to remember.

Doing my usual shopping on Christmas Eve, I ran across the judge at the mall.

"Did the tenants get their refunds yet?" Dave asked with a grin.

"Yessir. The party ran all night. Nobody wanted to quit."

"Well," he kept a perfectly straight face. "You know how we *schwartzas* are. Merry Christmas, Donovan."

Chapter 28

The casino land fever got worse by the day, but some things never change.

"Timmy, I've got to see you right away!" It was Sunday morning. When a phone call hits me on a Sunday morning, it's trouble. When it starts out with "Timmy", it's double trouble. Only old timers who knew me when the cops were listing broken street lights next to my name and confiscating my slingshot called me Timmy. Mrs. Madeline Dooley, well past 70 and mother of five of my contemporaries, had fed me too many cookies as a boy to feel awkward calling me on a Sunday morning. I agreed to meet her at the office in an hour. What the hell, maybe it *was* an emergency. The narrow escape I'd had with Anna Ruby as she lay on the hospital bed waiting for her will was still painfully fresh in my mind.

"I want to change my will," Mrs. Dooley announced after settling in to the green leather – covered wing chair I provided for my clients. An emergency! The dear old bat was good for 50,000 miles or 5 years, whichever came first. Like every other old lady I ever met, she could spot her lawn care guy fifty years and still outlive him. They don't get to be old ladies without survival skills, and once they've mastered them they go on forever. Still, I thought I'd double-check.

"Madeline, has the doctor given you bad news?"

"Eh? What's that? What locker? What badness?" she demanded in a loud voice. Among other annoyances, Mrs. Dooley's hearing had been going downhill for years but, with the independence of the truly bullheaded, she refused to give in and wear a hearing aid. I shouted the question again.

"Of course not! He's a damned quack anyway. They all are!"

"Then what's the emergency? Why do you have to change your will *today?*" I hoped the italics would remind her that it was, after all, Sunday. I'd done her will only a few months earlier. Aside from a minor item, she'd left everything to her children in equal shares. "Did you hit the lottery?"

"Pottery? What pottery?" she demanded. "Oh, you mean lottery! Speak up! Don't mumble. No, I don't waste money on that nonsense. It's all rigged anyway!" She dismissed millions of dollars of the State's lottery-hyping TV ads with a sniff and a shrug and got down to business. "Diane didn't invite me to dinner last night! And it was her birthday! Can you believe it?" Mrs. Dooley was as ticked off as only the mother of five grown children can be when feeling neglected by one of them.

"And now you want to cut her out of your will?" I'd had a rough Saturday night, and Sunday was seldom my best day for legal interviews. But this, I thought, was stretching things too far. Mrs. Dooley looked at me in disbelief. "Cut her out? Of course not! Who said anything about cutting her out? I want them to take equal shares. But I want the turtle to go to Frank!"

In her will, as in every such, there was a "Specific Bequests" clause. It's that part where you leave Grandmother's tablecloth to Daughter A and your rings to Daughter B and Grandpa's old fishing gear to little Johnny. Madeline's prize possession was her ceramic turtle. Accompanied by her cronies from the senior citizen's club, she'd taken up ceramics. After weeks of patient effort, she'd produced a large, richly colored turtle which, duly baked and glazed, was her pride and joy – the artistic zenith of a lifetime. This turtle – in her mind already a family heirloom to be passed down through the generations – she'd bequeathed to Diane, at that time the daughter who'd most recently taken her shopping. Parents do bribe children for their affection, even posthumously.

But Saturday had changed all that. If Diane was going to forget her own mother at Saturday night's birthday dinner, then the will must be changed on Sunday. Off the ceramic turtle went, by codicil, to Jeannette.

Codicils are easily drawn up, but someone has to type them, and the client has to come in for the signing, with witnesses standing by, all of which, however efficiently done, still costs. And even the most timid laborer gets paid for working on Sunday. But I'm a wimp when it comes to charging fees of old ladies who call me "Timmy", and Mrs. Dooley was the sort of snappish Irish dragon whose eyes lit up at the thought of imposing guilty feelings on Timmy the cookie-eater of years past. She would've paid, but an hour later she'd be down on her knees at church muttering loud prayers and lighting candles for my ungrateful soul. I never worked up the courage to charge her, and every few Sundays the call came through. For months that turtle traveled from Diane to Jeannette, from Jeannette to Frank, from Frank to Ed, from Ed to Jake, and back to Diane. My life became a nightmare of codicil Sundays, a treadmill on which I was doomed to shuffle for life, shackled to a ceramic turtle.

Then a miracle happened. The New Jersey legislature in its wisdom passed a new Law of Wills. Keep in mind it was in this same legislature that a member rose and, when asked "For what purpose does the gentleman rise?" uttered the immortal reply: "I rise to aerate my shorts!"

Folks don't expect much from the New Jersey legislature, which is why the change they made in the Law of Wills was such a wonderful surprise. No longer would it be necessary to do a new will or even a codicil for minor changes. The turtle could travel endlessly, now here, now there, and all that was needed to send it on its way was a simple, handwritten, signed note from Mrs. Dooley. No witnesses, no formalities, no need for a lawyer's intervention in so private a family matter.

Seldom, if ever, does anyone send flowers to the New Jersey State legislature, but I was tempted. Only at the last minute did I realize the arrival of flowers on the floor of the State Senate might be misinterpreted as a sign the Chief Justice had died, touching off a mad scramble for the job. People could get hurt, so I held back on the flowers. With almost childish glee I awaited the next Sunday call from Mrs. Dooley. It wasn't long in coming.

"Madeline," I shouted when we met, smiling my most winning smile, determined to charm the old dragon out of her socks. "I've great news!" I explained the new law that made things so easy for her. The look I got was somewhere between disdain and outright contempt.

"All I have to do is write a note?" she asked, her voice vibrant with suspicion of the law, the New Jersey legislature, and the ungrateful wretch who'd once eaten her cookies and was now trying to duck out of paying for them.

"That's all you have to do," I assured her.

"Hmmph! And this is one of those *new* laws?" She asked in a tone dismissive of any law passed since the Statute of Uses in 1272.

"A wonderful new law," I insisted. "Think how much easier it makes things for you."

The old battleaxe was unmoved. "So you say," she sniffed, stalling for time until she hit on the right strategy. "God knows what they'll come up with next. They tell me next year they'll be saying the Mass in English instead of Latin! Can you believe it?" Suddenly I was defending both the New Jersey legislature and the Vatican – a challenge no lawyer should be faced with after a rough Saturday night.

"But Madeline!" I protested.

No use. "That's all well and good for these young people," she said. "Thank God I've got you to depend on. You won't make me have to start writing letters and doing these new-fangled things, will you Timmy?"

I almost caved in. There's no coward in the world more craven than the man I see every morning in my mirror. But I was desperate and held my ground. Eventually she resigned herself to handwritten notes about the turtle. I don't know where that turtle ended up, but I firmly believe that when it came to rest, it must've breathed a heartfelt sigh of relief. I'm not sure whoever got it felt the same. How'd you like to wake up every morning with a glazed, bright-eyed turtle on your bedside table, assessing you with Mrs. Dooley's critical eye, deciding whether you were still worthy of its presence?

Chapter 29

Mark Twain said the two things people should never see being made are their sausages and their laws. Once the voters amended the State Constitution to legalize casinos in Atlantic City, it was up to the State Legislature to take care of the details. The process made a sausage factory look downright appetizing. Guys who'd been "rising to aerate their shorts" became instant experts on how many square feet of casino floor space you could build in exchange for each first-class hotel room you built; how many restaurants you had to have; whether the roulette wheels should have one zero or two; and how big the signs on the outside of the casinos should be.

The only thing they were dead certain about was that we were going to go first class. Forget that cheap, vulgar flash of Las Vegas. Atlantic City may have fallen on hard times but, by God, now we'd show the whole world what class looked like. James Bond, here we come.

And there'd be no crime. Whatever happened, organized crime wasn't gonna muscle in on our take. Everything and everybody connected with casinos would have to be fingerprinted, photographed, audited, investigated, probed, prodded and pronounced pure of heart and noble of mind before they could get a license to own, operate, sell to, or work for a casino. The process started by requiring everybody to fill out application forms and submit them to the new Division of Gaming Enforcement; an outfit known as the DGE.

The Casino Control Commission was a rubber stamp; a bunch of political appointees who were supposed to make the final decisions on whether anybody got a license. But the DGE had the investigators, state troopers, subpoena power, and money to dig up whatever dirt they could find on you. The hell of it was, when they finished digging, you had to pay the bill. If you'd worked in the Caribbean, Vegas, or other exotic climes where casinos were legal, the DGE snoops got to go on very nice vacations at your expense.

Once the dirt-diggers got done, the DGE's lawyers decided whether to oppose your license or let it go through. Since the Commission wasn't about to buck the DGE, your chance of getting work was in the DGE's hands. Of course, there was a certain hierarchy. Licensing of the big boys who owned and ran the casinos was handled by the DGE's top lawyers; guys who, over the years, coincidentally ended up as very well paid lawyers for the casinos they'd once investigated. Imagine that.

If you were a peasant hoping to deal cards, serve drinks, or mop floors, your right to work was handled by the junior flakes, flunkies and flyweights in little cubicles far down the hall. Since the number of non-casino jobs in Atlantic City other than cops, firemen, trash collectors and hookers was about 50, and the number of casino jobs was about 4,000 per casino, the bottom line was that you either made the dumbest hack in the DGE happy, or you could tap-dance on the Boardwalk for tips.

At the bottom of the DGE's legal food-chain was Ferdinand G. Gungham; the least competent lawyer with the smallest cubicle the farthest down the hall next to the men's room. Ferdie it was who designed the application forms for the lower classes, and Ferdie it was who decided if you were of pure character and spiritually suited for work in the casino industry. A smug, prissy twerp complete with sallow complexion, grating voice and the sense of humor of a dead mortician, Ferdie had managed to get through law school, pass the bar, get a legal flunky's job in Nixon's White House, and end up a junior lawyer for the DGE without ever once representing a client, meeting a judge, or trying a case. His training in character assessment came from being a gofer for guys like John Erlichman (you remember Erlichman; Nixon's top domestic policy advisor; left the White House to do 7 to 10 at Scottsdale Federal Minimum Security); Bob Haldeman (you remember Haldeman; Nixon's chief of staff; did 5 to 7 at Scottsdale); and Richard "I am not a crook" Nixon. (You remember Nixon.)

If anybody knew what bad character looked like, Ferdinand G. Gungham was the boy. He it was who got to design the application forms for the peasants looking for casino jobs. "Have you ever been convicted of a crime?" is fairly standard stuff, and he included it on the form. But Ferdie was grimly dedicated to covering all the bases. After the usual question about being convicted of a crime, he dreamed up the next question, which was: "Have you ever committed any act that would constitute a crime or misdemeanor even if you were never arrested for or accused of such offense?" Think of the guys at the White House answering that one, then or now.

This gem led to highly interesting results. A steady stream of cooks, janitors, cocktail waitresses, and would-be dealers came in for help filling out the forms. Keep in mind that at the time, sex between unmarried couples was, technically, still a crime or misdemeanor in a good many states. If you'd lived with your boyfriend in Connecticut, you'd committed an act that was a crime or misdemeanor.

"I have to put *that* on the form?" Patsy asked. She'd worked as a go-go dancer, an artist's model, and a cocktail waitress. Now she was hoping for a job serving drinks on the casino floor, where the tips were expected to be fabulous.

"The DGE says you gotta tell them. If you don't and they find out about it, that's ground for disqualification. Not the living together, but for not telling them."

"How they gonna find out about it?"

"Take a look at Question 77." It read: "List all persons with whom you have resided since the age of 15. Include family, friends, roommates, spouses, and co-workers."

Patsy wasn't happy, but she listed the long series of boyfriends with whom, over the years, she had lived. "Oh, God, the creeps I've

hooked up with! Half of them are probably wanted for something."
Eventually, we moved on to Question 85.

"List all birthmarks, scars, tattoos or other distinguishing marks on your body. Specify their location and briefly describe each mark."

"This is embarrassing," Patsy said.

"What's embarrassing?"

What was embarrassing was that at her boyfriend's urging one pot-smoking night she'd gotten the word "Welcome!" tattooed over what, for delicacy's sake, I'll call the lower portion of her abdomen.

"I have to write *that* down?"

"The Division says so. Also the pot-smoking."

"Donovan, what kind of weird fuckin' people dream up these questions?"

Having met Ferdie and several of his colleagues, I had to admit they were weird. Until you got to know them, when it became clear they'd left "weird" behind in high school and were now 23rd degree Assholes working their way up the ladder to perfection.

"What, I'm supposed to give some creeps my picture, my address, my phone number, and tell them I've got that tattoo? Screw it! I'll end up with every nut case in the government wanting to check it out personally." I taught her about the ever-handy "n/a" answer. Few things frustrate bureaucrats as much as finding an "n/a" in the blank spaces on forms. Does it mean "not applicable," "not available," or "not answering?" Are they being inconvenienced, ignored or, much worse, defied?

Using the experienced judgment of waitresses everywhere, she answered the tattoo question with "n/a." About three months later the Press carried the story of one of the DGE's investigators being arrested for stalking a young woman whose photo had caught his eye as he was processing applications. It wasn't Ferdie, but Patsy's gut instinct had been right on the money.

There are times when I've been somewhat critical of the local lawyers, but by and large they weren't a bad bunch. What they lacked in competence and moral turpitude they made up for with a certain *laissez faire* approach to other people's sins.

When it gradually dawned on them that their clients were being asked questions Torquemada wouldn't have tried at the Inquisition, they put up at least a token resistance. Some advised their clients to lie; others to leave the questions unanswered. One or two civil liberties types talked about challenging the nonsense in court – a challenge impossible to make because the casino industry doesn't hire people who make waves; and it certainly doesn't hire people who get the DGE pissed off. Even the most ardent civil liberties lawyers had trouble convincing clients they should fight the questionnaire. A job's a job, and if the government asks you to sign away your rights under the U.S. Constitution, the Bill of Rights, the New Jersey Constitution, and every other guarantee of those rights back to the Magna Carta, you don't argue. You close your eyes, hold your nose, and sign.

Even Bimbo did. It didn't seem to bother him. What did bother him and brought him into my office was when Ferdie came up with a recommendation that he be denied a license because he was a man of "unfit character." Just because he'd spent 30 years working in every mobbed-up casino from Stuebenville, Ohio to Havana, Cuba to Las Vegas was no reason to insult the man. I took the case.

What the hell, sooner or later somebody had to take Ferdinand G. Gungham down a peg or two. And Bimbo could pay; a factor which had increased in importance after a long dry spell.

Chapter 30

Most jobs have a career path that can be expressed in geography. Any diplomat's progress can be understood once you know he started out in Ouagadougou, moved on to Ulan Bator, then Buenos Aires, and onward and upward to Berlin, Paris, and London. A military guy who's been in Normandy, Inchon, Saigon and Central America doesn't have to tell you he's paid his professional dues. Casinos work the same way. Places like Steubenville, Ohio had hosted casinos run by the mob for years. They were illegal as hell, but offered the kind of hard-core casino experience treasured by casino owners anxious to recruit dealers who'd recognize the card-counters, wire-pullers, sleight-of-hand artists and other types that make profit margins so uncertain.

Like most young men of the day, Pasquale DeFortunato, also known as "Bimbo" for reasons he never revealed, had begun his working life in his hometown. It wasn't his fault his hometown was Steubenville.

As a kid he was paid to stand outside and keep an eye out for any trouble. By the time he was 15 he was a dealer. At 20 he was running roulette wheels in Havana in the days before Castro took over. At 25 Bugsy Siegel took him to Las Vegas.

Bimbo had worked, as he put it, "every jernt in town," in Vegas and Tahoe, and a number of "little jernts up the river," The picture became clearer when I figured out that a "jernt" was a "joint." Licensing was unheard of when he was a kid in Steubenville, except for the highly informal and unwritten agreements between cops and casinos that involved regular cash going out and undisturbed customers coming in. Much the same attitude prevailed in pre-Castro Havana, and by the time he got to Vegas Bugsy Siegel had things so organized you could arrive in town in the morning and be a licensed dealer working that afternoon.

Bimbo was a guy you liked right off. He was a short, thick-set man with a ready smile, a head of curly gray hair, eyebrows like raccoon tails, and brown eyes set in a leathery, deeply creased face that looked like a map of Sicily. He'd seen it all, never hurt anybody, and understood the casino world the way a commercial fisherman understands the sea. He didn't have to be taught, he kept his mouth shut about the way the boss ran things and who skimmed what, and like a surprising number of old-timers, quietly staked girls bus fare home if they looked too young to swim with the sharks.

Ferdie based his objection to Bimbo's license on two grounds: First, that he'd dealt cards at an illegal casino in Steubenville: Second, that five years ago he'd pleaded guilty to a gaming violation charge brought by the Nevada Gaming Commission.

Not much could be done about Steubenville. It was true, it happened 40 years earlier, and Bimbo had in any case been a juvenile when he worked there. Havana and Bugsy Siegel's Vegas, while raising eyebrows, were both legal and amounted at best only to guilt by association. The plea of guilty to a Nevada Gaming Board charge was more serious.

"I dunno nothin' about it," Bimbo protested.

"It says you pleaded guilty," I pointed to the DGE letter.

"Never heard of it." He shook his head in puzzlement. I believed him, but there it was – a copy of a Nevada charge against "one Pasquale DeFortunato, a/k/a 'Bimbo.' Disposition: Plea of Guilty. Fine $500."

"Do you remember paying a fine?" I asked.

"No. Like I say, I never heard of it." A lawyer's worst nightmare: A believable client who insists he's innocent.

"It says Club Nevada. You worked there?"

"Yeah. 'Bout three, four years. It's a little jernt up the river."

"What did you do at the jernt? I mean joint?"

"Everything. Ran the wheel, dealt blackjack and poker. Everything but the slots. It was a small jernt. Mostly locals."

I knew nobody in Nevada. But I did know Chuck McGinty at the Press. He contacted an editor of the one of the Nevada newspapers and got me the name of a reporter whose beat covered the Nevada Gaming Commission. In sales, they refer to it as a "cold call." You call the number, cross your fingers, and hope for the best. Luck was with me.

"Yeah, I know that joint. What's your guy's name? Pasquale DeFortunato? Doesn't ring a bell."

"How about Bimbo?"

"Bimbo! They're fuckin' *Bimbo* over?" He was incredulous. I explained Ferdie's objection.

"Donovan, what kind of weird fuckin' guys could object to Bimbo? He's been around forever!" The question had a familiar ring to it. With the reporter's help, I got through to the right guy in the Nevada Gaming Commission.

"Naw. Bimbo's okay. Why're they bustin' his chops?" I faxed him Ferdie's objections. He called back next morning.

"Off the record?"

"Absolutely."

"Okay. My buddy says his buddy says I can trust you."

"I'm good."

"Bimbo didn't know anything about it. Every year we make a sweep of the little joints so we look like we're not just picking on the big guys. Get 'em on some technical mistake. They plead guilty, pay the fine, and it's all over for another year."

"That's my problem. Bimbo pleaded guilty."

"Nah. He probably never even knew about it. What we do, we file the charge against the joint and mail the papers to the owner. He gives them to his lawyer, the lawyer calls us and negotiates a fine, the owner signs the plea and pays the fine. Odds are they never even told Bimbo."

"What was the charge?"

What Bimbo was alleged to have done was give free chips to a gambler – a no-no in Nevada at the time. I had Bimbo come in and read the charge.

"Nah, I never seen this. But it probably happened. A guy's at the table, piles up his chips and has to go take a leak. I don't wanna worry 'bout keepin' an eye on them, so I put them under the table where nobody's gonna steal them. Guy comes back, I give him back his stack. The Gaming Commission guy probably saw me give the guy back his chips, but didn't know I'd been lookin' after them for him. Wasn't a big deal."

"And nobody asked you about it? The Gaming Commission? The owner?"

Bimbo shrugged. "Don't matter. I'd have gone along with it anyway. They gotta get somethin' on the record just to prove they're doin' the job."

Remembering Atlantic City's annual Christmas raid on Sonia's and the end of season bust of gypsy fortune tellers, I could see his point of view. Next day I called Ferdie, certain that even he would concede that you can't keep a man out of a job based on charges he never saw, never knew about, and was innocent of in any event. Ferdie was unmoved.

"A plea's a plea. He was charged, a guilty plea was entered, a fine was paid. How do I know he didn't talk with that lawyer and admit he was guilty?"

"C'mon, Ferdie. Forty years in the industry and one highly dubious charge – "

"Forty years that included Steubenville, Havana, and Bugsy Siegel's casinos. The guy's got nothing going for him but some military service. I see no reason to withdraw the Division's objection."

I slammed down the phone thinking unkind thoughts. That sanctimonious bastard! Thinking he could judge a man's life by five minutes of it. It wasn't until the week before the hearing that the significance of Ferdie's words sank in – almost too late to follow up.

Chapter 31

L ife got a bit frenzied as the date for Bimbo's hearing before the Commission approached. Casino business was popping up everywhere; Mrs. Dooley got a ticket for running a red light; Joe Parsons had some unexpected problems; and I got my first out-of-town client.

Bob Salesses called from Washington – an old law school buddy whose bar-hopping habits had extended his contacts to half of Washington. Did I want to represent the Swiftline National Bus Company, who were anxious to protect their present Atlantic City monopoly against new competition for the casino business?

"Hell, yes!" He took a minute to let his eardrum stop vibrating, then got back on the phone.

"Okay. I'm setting it up with their Executive V.P. He's based in Houston, and wants to come to Atlantic City, meet you, and check things out. He's a little stuffy, but a good guy. Make sure you introduce him to all the right people."

The right people. My buddy wasn't exactly up to date on Atlantic City. The "right people" if you wanted to do business with casinos included, among others, Triple Dip, with whom I was on terms of mutual contempt owing to his suspicion that I had something to do with scuttling the minimum fee schedule; and Barry Stewart of Pirate Porn fame, who hated my guts for making an ass out of him in the

YMCA case. The only people I could impress my prospective client with were the hookers, former drug addicts, and tattooed waitresses of Atlantic City. Even First Count had retired, deciding he'd had enough investigating and was looking for something less strenuous.

Still, one does what one can. I blew the bankroll on a Navy blue pin-striped suit from Brooks Brothers, a crisp white shirt, regimental tie, and black wingtips from Bally of Switzerland. It was a rig bound to impress the highest executive Houston could send.

The big day arrived. My secretary served coffee in my freshly-cleaned office. We discussed the ins and outs of the casino industry, and promptly at noon set out for lunch. Sam the rabbi was to join us, and had promised to bring along the Mayor, who had not yet been indicted. Harry Castleman rode down the elevator with us. He eyed my new suit with a distinct air of approval. Maybe I'd make something of myself yet. I introduced him to the Houston V.P. Harry nodded gravely and congratulated him on getting so brilliant a lawyer to represent him. He said that with a perfectly straight face.

We rounded the corner, walking the few blocks to the restaurant. One or two friends seemed a bit startled by my Brooks Brothers get-up, but nobody gave the game away. Then came a loud squeal of brakes, an unmistakable whiff of *Eue d'Garbage*, and a loud shout. "My man!" Joe Parsons swung down from the trash truck and gave me a great hug. "How's it goin'?"

I introduced him to the Houston V.P. Joe gave him a high five. "Best lawyer in town, man! He lookin' after you, you gonna be fine!"

"How's Cynthia?" I asked.

"Oh, man," Joe moaned. "I got my ass in such trouble with that woman!"

"Trouble? With Cynthia? What happened?" My client stood politely back, but getting out of range of Joe's voice couldn't be done without a taxi.

"Well, you know I been layin' up with Julia?" I hadn't known, but Julia, who lived only a few doors from Joe, was a good-looking woman. Apparently she had a bit of First Count's easy attitude about sex in her genetic makeup.

"Yeah?" I asked.

"Well, I was at Julia's one night, drinkin' wine, smokin' dope, and listenin' to some Ahmed Jamal-man, that sucker's cool! Then I went home and Cynthia jumped all over my ass the minute I walked in the bedroom!"

"How'd she know?" I asked. Houston edged forward to hear the details.

"Man, I'm the dumbest son of a bitch!" Joe laughed. "I had my shorts on outside my pants! An' I couldn't think of nothin' to say! I hadda send that woman to the Islands for three weeks just to get her off my case!"

I didn't think Houston was overly impressed with his prospective lawyer. But we got through lunch okay. After meeting the Mayor and enjoying a few stiff drinks, he let out a chuckle.

"You know," he laughed, "I've been thinking it over, and damned if I could have thought of anything to say either!"

Chapter 32

I had to squeeze in one more case before the hearing on Bimbo's licensing. Mrs. Dooley had been driving to Philly when she came to Egg Harbor City's one and only traffic light. It was yellow, she was thinking of who should get the turtle in her next revision, and the rookie cop, freshly inspired by the latest Clint Eastwood movie, decided Mrs. Dooley had made his day. She made it even more when he switched on his siren. She couldn't hear it, kept driving, and was outraged when he forced her over to the side and issued her tickets for ignoring the traffic light and "eluding the arresting officer."

"The nerve!" Mrs. Dooley fumed as we drove to court. "If he wanted me to stop, why didn't he turn his siren on?"

There are cases that can make or break a lawyer's career. This was one of them. Either I helped Mrs. Dooley beat the rap, or my name was mud among all the potential clients for whom her cakes had shown up at weddings, baptisms, graduations and funerals.

Egg Harbor is, as its one traffic light suggests, a small town. It sits in the Jersey pinelands, 20 miles west of Atlantic City, astride the White Horse Pike which stretches between Atlantic City and Philadelphia. Like many small towns, Egg Harbor pays close attention to its solitary traffic light. It's a nice little money-maker that helps keep taxes down. Cars traveling North-South are invariably locals and seldom get ticketed.

Those traveling East-West are heading from Atlantic City to Philadelphia, or *vice versa,* and are fair game. Few motorists from either place drive to Egg Harbor's monthly court session to contest their tickets.

Mrs. Dooley took a different view. She considered any traffic ticket issued to law-abiding old ladies a form of persecution. Might as well be Russia! Put up a traffic light that changes from green to red in the blink of an eye, and then ticket honest citizens who'd been driving since certain cops were in diapers! I sternly advised her to keep calm when we got to court sand to let me do the talking.

The court met in a hall over the firehouse. The hall, when not in use as a court, served as the training, recreation, and fund-raising center for the volunteer fire company. As such, it sported a pool table, a bar, dartboard, shuffleboard, and various mounted moose heads and fish hung on the walls. Joe Kleffman, one of the few indisputably honest township judges, had a face like Spencer Tracy in his later years. He sat the fourth Wednesday of every month, hearing an ever more crowded docket. The closer we got to the casinos opening, the more traffic flowed through his town and the busier his court got. In addition to the traffic-light business, he had the usual array of barroom brawls, domestic violence, public drunkenness and miscellaneous disorderly conduct cases to hear and decide.

"What happened to the deer?" he asked the young man who'd just pleaded guilty to shooting deer out of season.

"We're still eatin' off it," the defendant answered.

"Still eatin' off the deer?"

"Had to. It was that or go on welfare. Couldn't get no job." Kleffman's plain and honest face was troubled. Here was a young man who'd done nothing wrong but kill a deer to feed his family and keep off welfare. Illegal, but Joe Kleffman shared the views of the community that had chosen him to be its judge.

"Well, you can't go shootin' deer out of season," he pointed out. "It's illegal. If you can't find work, you're not supposed to go around breaking the law. You're supposed to go on welfare. That's what it's for." He said the words, but his heart clearly wasn't in it and the crowd knew it.

"Won't have to now, Judge. Got a job yesterday layin' fiberglass at the boat works."

The judge's brow cleared. "All right, then. I'll impose a hundred dollar fine and fifty dollars costs. Suspend the fine and costs on condition you don't shoot any more deer until the season starts. Understand?"

"Yes, Sir."

"Okay. Next case." He looked down to make a note on the back of the deer ticket.

"State versus Madeline Dooley!" announced the clerk. "Red light, and eluding arrest."

The judge looked up. His eyebrows rose slowly as Mrs. Dooley and I approached the defense table. An old lady, eluding arrest? He looked at the rookie cop quizzically as the clerk administered him the oath. Mrs. Dooley, unbowed and unimpressed by police, traffic lights, and courts, glared at the rookie with undisguised contempt. I entered a plea of "Not Guilty." They were the last words I was able to get in.

"What happened?" The judge asked the rookie. Madeline caught the "what happened?" but ignored the rookie's attempt to answer.

"He's got nothin' better to do than give tickets to old ladies!" she announced. "He oughta be ashamed of hisself! He don't have enough to do, all he has to do is set there eating doughnuts and waiting for innocent citizens to give tickets to!"

Judge Kleffman banged the gavel. "Mr. Donovan, have your client keep quiet. She'll get her turn."

"Burn? What burn? I didn't get no burn! I got a ticket! That light was green and that boy," she spat the word with contempt, "that boy should be ashamed of hisself!"

The judge looked at me. I shrugged my shoulders. If there was anything clear as daylight, it was that nothing short of physical force was going to shut Mrs. Dooley up, and the odds weren't good even that would do the job. He looked over the crowded room, a month's worth of cases waiting to be heard, all enjoying the moment; took another look at Mrs. Dooley and, with the experience of years on the bench, banged his gavel. "Not Guilty!" he said. "Next case!"

The rookie, who had yet to give a word of testimony, looked around for help. The judge waved him off the stand impatiently.

"Guilty! Did he say I was guilty?" Madeline demanded.

"NOT guilty!" I shouted, grabbing my briefcase. "He said you're NOT guilty! Let's go!"

"Oh," she said, vaguely disappointed. The blood of a thousand Irish kings flowed through the Dooley veins, and here a good fight had ended before she could get warmed up. "I guess that's different. Although why they let little boys like that bother old ladies like me is beyond me!"

I gave the judge a pleading glance to give me a fair chance to get her out of his courtroom. He nodded in recognition of my problem as I maneuvered the still-grumbling Mrs. Dooley out of earshot.

"You're a good lawyer, Timmy!" she said when I dropped her off at home. "Come around tomorrow and I'll have a cake for you."

And they wonder why the Irish drink!

Chapter 33

"The important thing," Ferdie told the Commission, "is that a license to work in a casino isn't a right at all. It's a privilege. And the State can condition that privilege as it wishes. In this case the standard set for a license is that the applicant shall be – and I quote – 'of fit character.' As this record shows," he finished with a flourish, "Mr. DeFortunato is clearly lacking in character. The Division recommends that his license be denied."

The Chairman and his four fellow commissioners looked suitably bored. A rubber stamp has few exciting moments in life. It was plain that Steubenville, Havana, Bugsy Siegel and the incident at the little jernt up the river could sink Bimbo's chance beyond hope of salvage. But Ferdie had really pissed me off. There's a snide tone of voice no self-respecting lawyer should accept. And certain legal propositions should be fought until we beat them.

American democracy has fallen victim to three great scams. The first is that corporations are legally "persons," as entitled to the full protection of the Constitution as you and I. But corporations can't be drafted, can't vote, and never die. So this nonsense does nothing but shift human rights to an inhuman collection of stocks, bonds and proxies. The second scam is that class warfare is undemocratic. The result is the guys at the top keep stealing the pensions and poisoning the lungs of those below, then scream "class warfare!" when the little guys try to get back some of their own by raising taxes on the rich.

The third scam is that licenses are not rights, but privileges. By saying your driver's license is a privilege and not a right, the state can therefore yank it away from you without benefit of a jury trial. According to state law, a license to mop floors in a casino was a privilege and, therefore, the State in the person of Ferdinand G. Gungham could insist you sign away all your real rights as a condition of enjoying the privilege of a decent job – then deny you the license anyway!

I took on the problem from the little jernt up the river first, producing a letter from the casino's lawyer confirming that Bimbo had never been informed of the charge, never personally had a chance to contest it, and never had pleaded or authorized a plea of guilty. That had about the same effect on the stone-faced Commissioners as throwing snowballs at statues, but at least I'd put it on the record.

Then I did what I could to shake things up.

"Counsel is correct," I told the Commissioners, Bimbo at my side. "My client is an unfit character in several ways." Whatever else happened, I got their attention. The rubber stamp perked up its collective ears.

"He is, for one thing, a product of the mob." The Commissioners were shuffling through their copies of the file, trying to get my name straight. "How else can I explain his going to work at the age of 15 as a dealer in an illegal, mob-run casino in Steubenville, Ohio? The fact that working in that casino was the only job he could land during the Depression, and that his earnings helped feed his mother and three little sisters doesn't excuse him. If he had the right character, he'd have let them go hungry rather than take the same kind of job you hope to create in Atlantic City by the thousands." Five puzzled faces looked down on me. It was beginning to dawn on them that maybe the DGE had led them into a swamp. What's wrong with a 15-year-old kid getting a job?

"For another thing, he's certainly a liar. A demonstrable, confirmed, indisputable liar!"

Now I not only had their attention, but the television cameramen who'd been standing by waiting to catch the bigger fish later that morning started bustling around plugging stuff in and turning on lights. "A liar," I continued, "at a young age. When he was 15 he was already corrupt, working for the mob. But my friend," I turned to Ferdie, pure acid in my voice, "doesn't do his case justice. No. It's not enough to brand him incorrigibly corrupt because at the age of 15 he got a casino job to help support his widowed mother and his little sisters. He did far worse than that!"

A pin dropping would have sounded like the atomic bomb.

"He lied to his own government! And he lied under oath!" I reached into my briefcase for the document received only that morning. "Here," I brandished the paper, "is a certified photostatic copy of that lie. On Monday morning, December 8, 1941, my client presented himself at the United States Marine Corps recruiting station in Chicago, waited hours in line, and wilfully and deliberately perjured himself about his age so he could join the Marine Corps at the age of 15!"

Ferdie began to squirm. The Commissioners, three of them combat veterans, were sitting on the edge of their chairs.

"Having lied about his age," I continued, "my client went off to boot camp. From there he was sent to the South Pacific, where he celebrated his 16th birthday and, still living that wicked lie that he was old enough, took part in the assaults on those Japanese-held islands in which so many Marines shed their blood."

"There came a day when he was still 16," I was not about to let Ferdie and his hypocritical privileges out of my grip, "when he was ordered with his fellow Marines to capture the island of Guadalcanal. Shall I read what the military archives say about his character in that battle?"

The Chairman, who'd spent painful days pinned under enemy fire at Anzio, nodded.

"Corporal DeFortunato," I read from the war record retrieved from the military archives at St. Louis, "served as a squad leader of Marine Company C, Third Battalion, in the assault on Guadalcanal. In that action," I read, "eight of his squad members were killed. Another was seriously wounded. When the Chaplain crawled forward to administer the Sacraments, he, too, was wounded. Corporal DeFortunato, under heavy enemy fire, crawled forward to rescue his wounded squad member. In doing so he himself was hit in the leg by enemy fire. Notwithstanding his wound, he pulled his fellow Marine to safety. Having rescued his man, he went back to rescue the wounded Chaplain. On that final rescue he was hit twice more by enemy fire; once in the hip and once in the thigh. He persevered, and brought the Chaplain back to safety."

"I can read more," I said. "But that should be sufficient." Ferdie rose to respond, caught the angry flash of the Chairman's glare, and sat down. The Commission voted unanimously to stick it to the DGE and grant Bimbo his license.

Chapter 34

Ferdie backed off considerably after that. He holed up in his cubicle, licked his wounds and kept a low profile. His bosses at the DGE blamed him for the newly changed attitude of the Commissioners, who had thrown away their rubber stamps and were now treating DGE license objections with a healthy skepticism.

Bimbo's case brought other unexpected benefits. Triple Dip and Norman Kartman had been in the Marine Corps together in Korea. Now they represented the top casino owners, who were coming up for licensing. They'd been in the room when I'd hammered the DGE with the record of Bimbo's heroism at Guadalcanal. Norman's bravery in the Marine Corps was legendary, and Triple Dip, for all his faults, was still carrying lead in his shoulder from Inchon. Like all Marines their loyalty to the Corps was a lifetime commitment. My beating up the DGE on behalf of a Marine as gutsy as Bimbo put me on the side of the angels as far as they were concerned.

"Good work, Donovan," Triple Dip congratulated me. "It was about time somebody kicked those bastards in the balls." Whatever softened up the DGE was okay in his book.

"Hell of a job, Donovan," I'd last seen Norman at the YMCA Bankruptcy trial, when we parted on somewhat less than friendly terms.

He patted me on the back as I left the room. "Anything I can do for you, let me know."

"I could use an introduction to your client," I said. He was personal counsel to *Bonne Chance's* Board Chairman, a man who could decide whether the Swiftline National Bus Company got exclusive rights to run to the casino when it opened. I explained my interest.

"You got it," Norman said. "I'll set up a lunch."

Triple Dip, who represented *Bonne Chance* as a corporation, grabbed my arm on the way out. "Norm will put you in tight with the Chairman," he said. "And I'll bring along the operating guys. No reason we can't get your man an exclusive."

I struck while the iron was hot. "Listen, Trip – er, Danny. What I could really use are tickets to the opening night show for my clients." *Bonne Chance* had announced plans for a gala opening – black tie dinner, celebrity show, VIP's everywhere. The media coverage would be heavy. If I could get Houston a ticket to the opening, I'd be in clover.

"I can do better than that," Triple Dip never did things by halves. "You'll have a table for ten. On the house!" For a moment I was touched, forgetting Triple Dip's basic philosophy. "Where they gonna park those buses?" he continued. "If you and I buy some ground, we can rent it to them as a parking lot. We'll bang 'em for $50 a bus. They won't scream because they can bill my client for it. I'll see my client goes along, then you and I can split the take!" His eyes shone with heartfelt enthusiasm at the thought of skimming a little here, a little there. Happily interrupted by the general exodus from the hearing room, I mumbled something about getting back to him later and made good my escape.

Sure enough, a few weeks later ten engraved invitations arrived. I called Houston, got the name of the other executives he'd be bringing, and the names of their wives. I lined up the fast – disappearing hotel rooms they'd need, ordered orchids for the ladies, and rented myself a tux.

Meanwhile, Bimbo's story had gotten around in Vegas, where everybody in town knew him. Half of Vegas wanted jobs in the new Atlantic City. My calender filled up with guys of long experience but shaky reputations in need of an Atlantic City lawyer who could get them past Ferdie and the DGE.

The buzz of activity in town was turning into a loud roar of frenzied last-minute efforts to get ready for opening day. The Governor, every politician above the rank of dogcatcher, and fat guys with names like Big Sid who owned waste-hauling businesses were planning to come. The thing grew and grew as we approached C-Day.

"Gonna be a fuckin' nuthouse!" Jack Jenner told me. He and his motorcycle had been taken off their regular beat and assigned to handle the expected traffic crunch.

At last came the big day – the grand opening of the *Bonne Chance* Casino-Hotel. The ribbon cutting was set for six o'clock. By the time the Governor cut the ribbon, the scene looked like a cross between the Oscar awards and the Superbowl. Long, sleek limousines slipped between television trucks, taxi's, and hordes of pedestrians. The line waiting outside to get in was twenty abreast and stretched five blocks down the Boardwalk. The experts had predicted an opening day crowd of 10,000. More than 250,000 showed up.

With smooth cunning and Jack Jenner's help, I arranged for our limousine to drop my little group off at a back entrance. Here we were, tuxedoed, flowered, limousined, and escorted by a police motorcycle complete with flashing light and wailing siren. All through dinner and the opening show visions of glory danced in my head. I saw myself in a few more hours as Sean Connery, leaning suavely over the Baccarat table and saying "Banco!" By the end of an evening like this, I'd have my clients so impressed they'd be recommending me to half the oil men in Houston. Before long I'd probably be handling international clients. Which would make more sense, I pondered: Should I buy a private jet, or just lease it? Lease, I decided. Only way to go.

After dinner, our table and the other thousand or so elegantly dressed guests were politely guided out of the theater and down a lushly carpeted hallway to the double doors that led to the casino floor.

"Which shall it be first," I asked Mrs. Executive V.P., whose hairdo cost more than my average fee for a traffic case. "Baccarat or Blackjack?"

"Oh, Baccarat," she smiled. I pushed open the door and stepped back to let my clients go ahead.

It would probably have been better had I gone first. Maybe I could have grabbed the drunk before he tripped into her, spilling his beer down the front of her gown. Unable to stop because of the crush of a thousand guests behind us eager to get to the tables, she stumbled down the step and disappeared into the crowd. It was the last I ever saw of her, her husband, or the rest of my small party. They were swallowed up by the surging masses, pushed deep into the mob by the procession behind.

Dazed but nimble, my ears slowly adjusted to the unholy din of raised voices, jangling coins, and slot machines. I bulled my way to the side where, my back safely against the wall, I scanned the mob frantically for my clients. I saw a flash of a gown here and a tuxedo there, but couldn't tell if they were my group or the remnants of the elegantly-clothed column of VIP's that was rapidly being absorbed by the thousands of gamblers in tee shirts, blue jeans, jogging suits and mu-mu's milling around, trying to capture seats at the blackjack tables by main force. The column of tuxedoed guests disappeared like the lost legions of Varus among the Teutonic barbarians.

The present barbarians were an enthusiastic bunch, I'll say that for them. After an hour of intense effort I gave up the search for my lost clients – and my dreams of private jets. The crowd had, if anything, grown. I moved a few inches and stubbed my toe on something.

"Watch yer fuckin' step, willya?" came an angry yell. I looked down. There, jammed against a pillar next to a blackjack table, a guy with no legs and one arm lay belly-down on a four-wheeled dolly, wearing a grimy tee-shirt, some kind of jeans, and a three day growth of beard. His buddy, holding down a seat at the table, reached down and gave him a drag of his cigarette.

"Got a queen an' a six. Dealer's got a jack an' a five. Take a hit?"

"Fuck, yeah!" came instructions from below. The push of the current carried me away before I could see how he made out.

Another half-hour's jostling got me past the slots. I caught a glimpse of the Baccarat table, but had more or less lost the James Bond spirit by then and was more in the elbows and kneecap mode necessary for surviving on the casino floor. Coming to rest against another pillar, I was calculating whether to try bulling my way across the main floor to an exit, or work my way around the walls 'till I got there, when I felt a tug at my elbow.

"How you doin', Mr. Donovan?" It was First Count. And unless I was hallucinating, he was wearing a plastic badge with his picture on it and "Cleared for Cash" printed under his name.

"First Count! How the hell did you land that job? I thought getting licensed to handle cash was almost impossible!" There were licenses of every kind. One license for cooks, another for dishwashers, separate ones for janitors, waitresses, even the guys who delivered the bread. I knew from hard-won experience everybody had to fill out those 30-page applications and go through a clearance, including Ferdie, that would've made the KGB jealous. Yet here was First Count, shiny plastic credentials pinned to his lapel, not only licensed but fully accredited to handle the cash! Where the hell was Ferdie when they needed him?

First Count nodded with a pleased smile. "Yes, sir, Mr. Donovan. It's pretty bad. Folks are having to wait and wait. Matter of fact, we only got 15 people licensed to handle the cash, and it looks like we could use 'bout ten times that!"

He was obviously right about that. The effect of Ferdie's chickenshit scrutinizing of license applications had gummed up the works beyond belief. There weren't nearly enough licensed staff for the mob. What staff they had was overwhelmed. There wasn't an inch of room on the floor. People stood three and four deep at the slot machines, and the bars were so crowded you could've walked across the heads of waiting customers. Bartenders were shrugging off $10 tips and serving only those pushing $20 bills under their noses. Cocktail waitresses who were supposed to be serving free drinks to the blackjack players were being handed $20 bills per drink before they could get anywhere near the tables. The slot machines were taking in money so fast the bucket-emptiers couldn't keep up. With so few employees licensed to handle the cash, *Bonne Chance*'s Chairman of the Board was in his shirtsleeves, hauling buckets of quarters to the hard-count room like a coal miner getting paid by the ton.

First Count stood diplomatically out of sight, between me and an exit door.

"So how'd you get licensed?" I asked again.

"You know," he smiled, "all those years I been nice to the ladies? It paid off. One of them got a job handling the license applications. She helped me fill it out and got it through. I was the 11th man licensed to handle cash. I don't do no heavy liftin', though," he watched the Chairman sweating as he hefted another bucket of quarters. "I handle the soft count. Jes' paper money."

I couldn't help but laugh. "So how are they to work for?"

"Oh, fine," he chuckled. "Just fine! We had a big meetin' when we got hired and they had the Chairman of the Board – that's him over there – come talk with us just like I'm standin' here talking to you. He said he didn't want us feelin' like employees. Said we should think of ourselves as partners."

"Partners! First Count, do they have any idea how you got your nickname?" His nickname came from following his daddy's advice that "it don't matter who your partner is, so long as you get first count of the money!"

He pursed his lips and looked around. "Well, now about that, I'd appreciate if you'd keep quiet 'bout that 'First Count' business. Everybody here calls me 'Baby.'"

"That doesn't mean you've forgotten your father's advice, does it?" I asked, tongue in cheek.

His eyes gleamed. "No sir, Mr. Donovan. But he give me some other advice back then.He said what your partner don't know can't hurt you. 'Scuse me now, Mr. Donovan," his smile widened, "I gotta go hold up my end of the partnership." I watched him slip behind the dealer at a nearby blackjack table. He emptied a cash box stuffed with hundred dollar bills into a canvas sack, then worked his way around the tables in the pit, emerging with the sack brimming over with the take. Nobody signed receipts for anything. The dealers where happy to have the boxes emptied so they had room to stuff in more hundred dollar bills. First Count moved off with a smile and the bag full of hundreds while the Chairman of the Board struggled manfully to hoist another bucket full of quarters onto a cart. Partners! With First Count as his partner and Triple Dip as his lawyer, the Chairman'd be lucky if he got to keep the quarters. I shook my head and started to fight my way through the crowd to the exit. Suddenly a gravelly, booming, unforgettable voice came through the din.

"Yeah, I wanna hit! How'm I gonna make money standin' on 16?" I turned just in time to watch Big Dingy, dressed in an elegant tuxedo but as impassive as ever, deal a 5 to Shipyard, then push his winning chips to him.

It was several months later when, feeling the pinch because I still hadn't received my check from the Public Defender for the Skin Game trial, I called Bob LeBreaux to find out what the problem was. He called back in an hour. "No problem, Donovan. I called Trenton. They promised to get a check to you next week."

"Thanks. Nothing like work now, eat next year."

"They say your man's taking an appeal."

"He won't have a snowball's chance in hell, but good luck to him. What grounds is he going on?"

"Claims his trial counsel was incompetent." LeBreaux had a wicked sense of mischief.

"He what? Why, that son of a bitch!"

"Well, you told him that was your first jury trial, didn't you?" LeBreaux was still laughing when he hung up. I tried working up a head of steam, but LeBreaux was right. All I could do was laugh. Frank had me from the get-go, and knew it. What the hell, the man was appealing prison sentences while I was still in grade school.

Wonder if Bill Cosby wants the part?

Acknowledgments

There are books that require their authors to thank librarians, sources and researchers by the score. This is not one of them. For the raw material I thank the everyday but not-very-ordinary people of Atlantic City. All else that was needed was moral support, for which I thank the many who gave it; an editorial eye, for which I thank Louis Toscano; and a place to write, for which I am ever-grateful to Dr. Marta Rozans, known as "Dr. Cookie" to her young patients in Pediatric Oncology at Tulane Medical Center, who shared her home, her family and her New Orleans with endless patience and contagious enthusiasm.

The cover art is the work of Joyce Dougherty, graphics designer *extraordinaire*, whose services were generously made available by Alan and David Kligerman at AkPharma, Inc.

To contact the Author by e-mail: *wilkins1@att.net*